THE GREAT ESCAPE

THE GREAT ESCAPE

DR. KATE BIBERDORF
WITH HILLARY HOMZIE

Philomel Books

Hi! My Name is DR. Kate Biberdorf,

but most people call me Kate the Chemist. I perform explosive science experiments on national TV when I'm not in Austin, Texas, teaching chemistry classes. Besides being the best science in the entire world, chemistry is the study of energy and matter, and their interactions with each other. Like how I can use dry ice to make a Ghost or baking soda to make Moon Rocks! If you read *The Great Escape* carefully, you will see how Little Kate the Chemist uses chemistry to solve problems in her everyday life.

But remember, none of the experiments in this book should be done without the supervision of a trained professional! If you are looking for some fun, safe, at-home experiments, check out my companion book, *Kate the Chemist: The Big Book of Experiments*. (I've included one experiment from that book in the back of this one—how to make magnetic slime!)

And one more thing: Science is all about making predictions (or forming hypotheses), which you can do right now! Will Little Kate the Chemist and her friends make it out of the escape room in time? Let's find out—it's time for Kate the Chemist's second adventure.

XOXO,
Kate

PHILOMEL BOOKS
An imprint of Penguin Random House LLC, New York

First published in the United States of America by Philomel,
an imprint of Penguin Random House LLC, 2020.

Visit us online at penguinrandomhouse.com

Library of Congress Cataloging-in-Publication Data is available.

Printed in the United States of America

ISBN 9780593116586

1 3 5 7 9 10 8 6 4 2

Edited by Jill Santopolo. Design by Lori Thorn.
Text set in ITC Stone Serif.

This book is dedicated to my niece, Q.
Escape the ordinary.

CONTENTS

CHAPTER ONE

GEttiNG SPOOKED

Beaker (noun). A glass piece of equipment used to hold chemicals. It's used to store and pour things and is heat, cold, and crack resistant. It's made from a super-strong type of glass, almost like a superhero glass.

"WHO'S READY TO UNLEASH some ghosts?" asked Ms. Daly.

"I am!" My feet bounced, along with my ponytail. And every atom in my body. We weren't going to release real ghosts though. Actual spooky stuff scares me.

Instead, we were going to create ghosts in our science lab at school.

Ms. Daly stood in the front of the class in her blue

lab coat, safety goggles around her neck. "Don't forget to put on your gloves," she said. "This might be a competition, but safety comes first."

Ms. Daly was teaching a special week of science classes for our Fall Science Challenge. She's a retired air force flight engineer. Normally, she's in charge of the after-school chemistry club, which I never *ever* miss, but this week she was there during the school day, too.

"It's show time!" Ms. Daly pulled on her goggles, adjusting the strap around her short silver hair.

Plucking a stopwatch out of her pocket, she peered out at the nine of us. Basically half of my fifth-grade class. While we were doing the Fall Science Challenge, the other half of my class was drumming with Mr. Graham. It would be our turn to drum tomorrow.

"Okay, in your places," said Ms. Daly. "We're going to start in three minutes. All the materials are right here." She pointed to a rectangular table next to her filled with things like plastic soda bottles, food coloring, baking soda, and lemons.

Thrusting my chin forward, I checked out the supplies and wondered what to expect. I had to be prepared for anything. The Ghost was our first challenge, followed by something called Moon Rocks, and then Neon Brains.

"Jeremy's team already has their bottle," called out Phoenix Altman, who was on my team. "That's definitely not fair!"

"I agree," said Julia Yoon from the table diagonally across from ours.

Everyone's eyes zoomed in on Jeremy Rowe. He's hard to miss, because he's big with a purple streak in his blond hair. Arms folded, he stood next to his teammates, Memito Alvarez and Elijah Williams. The three blinked as if someone had taken a photo with a really bright flash.

"Boys, I strongly suggest you put the bottle back," said Ms. Daly in a firm voice.

Brushing a curl off his forehead, Jeremy said extra sweetly, "I didn't know we weren't supposed to take it yet." Sometimes he charms teachers, but luckily Ms. Daly doesn't fall for stuff like that.

"Cheating makes me so mad," I said under my breath to my teammates, Birdie Bhatt and Phoenix.

"I can't believe he thought he could get away with it," whispered Birdie, who happens to be my very best friend.

"I can," Phoenix said, fiddling with the macramé bracelet on her wrist. "Jeremy makes up his own rules." Smoothing her tie-dye shirt, she sighed dramatically.

"Boys," said Ms. Daly. "If you don't put back what you took, your grade will suffer."

Memito smacked the bottle into Jeremy's hand. "Dude, hurry," Memito whispered with a worried frown. But Jeremy just strolled back toward the equipment table. Meanwhile, his teammate Elijah peered up at a poster about molecules. He's my other best friend, and I know he'd never purposefully cheat.

"Mr. Rowe, you're moving slower than pond water." Ms. Daly waved her glove-covered hand. "You wouldn't want to be the cause of your team being disqualified from winning the prize, would you?"

All at once, Jeremy zipped across the floor. Then he banged down the bottle. "That prize is going to be ours," he announced all matter-of-factly.

"Sorry, but FYI, that's going to be

our team," said Julia, crossing her arms. She is student council president and knows a thing or two about winning. She flicked her eyes knowingly at her teammates, Avery Cooper and Skyler Rumsky, the tallest and also quietest boy in the fifth grade.

"Actually, it's going to be us." I curled my arms around Birdie and Phoenix. I really wanted our team to win the prize—the chance to do the Vomiting Pumpkin demo at the Fall Festival this weekend. This year is our last Fall Festival at Franklin, since we'll be in middle school next year. So it's got to be epic.

And yes, the demo is as cool and disgusting as it sounds. Green foaming goop oozes out of a jack-o'-lantern's mouth. I've seen Dr. Caroline, my favorite chemist, do it on YouTube.

I hoped that the Ghost we were about to make for the Fall Science Challenge would be just as awesome.

I had been looking forward to the Science Challenge for weeks.

All right, months.

It was a tradition at Rosalind Franklin Elementary School. It came right before the Fall Festival, so in my opinion, it was the very best time of the year. Why?

Well, some kids are into stuffed animal collections.

Others are into certain video games. Or art, like my BFF Birdie.

I—Kate Crawford—am all about science, especially chemistry. I was so ready to start that my mouth watered.

You see, I wasn't just ready to start the Science Challenge. I was ready to win it.

CHAPTER TWO

SOMETHING STINKS!

Compound (noun). A compound is a substance made when two or more elements are bonded together. Like how hydrogen hitches with oxygen to form water or when besties hold hands and skip down the hallway. They become a united team—Best Friends Forever ♥

"OKAY, YOU HAVE FIFTEEN SECONDS before the challenge begins," said Ms. Daly. "Be prepared to read the directions on your index cards."

Kids snapped their goggles onto their heads. Mine were a little too tight, but I'd just have to deal with it.

"Ready, set, you bet!" called out Ms. Daly.

Everyone flipped over the index card with the directions for how to make the Ghost.

"Why don't you read it aloud," I suggested to Phoenix. "Birdie and I will grab what we need."

After drawing in a deep breath, Phoenix read dramatically. "The goal is to make a spooky Ghost that reaches the finish line."

"What finish line?" I said, glancing around the science lab. "Where?"

Birdie gazed up, and a smile grew on her face. "Up there!" she pointed.

The other two teams focused on the ceiling, where yellow crepe paper hung from one side of the room to the other.

"Aha!" I whispered. "Now I get it."

"In order to complete this challenge and go on to Moon Rocks," continued Ms. Daly, "your Ghost must touch the yellow line. Remember to pick up your supplies here."

She pointed to the table next to a large potted cactus.

"Our Ghost's going to get a gold medal," said Jeremy, twirling his pointer finger like he was number one.

"Correction," said Julia. "That would be ours."

"More like ours," I said. "And ours is going to be like Casper, a very friendly ghost."

Elijah giggled, Memito shook his head, and Jeremy smirked.

Phoenix plunked her hands on her hips. I could tell she was as serious as I was about the competition. And just as annoyed at Jeremy, too.

Meanwhile Birdie kept on peering up at the ceiling with a dreamy expression. She's an artist, so it didn't faze me too much. I'm definitely used to the ways of my BFF.

"Keep reading, please," I urged Phoenix. "Hurry."

"Okay." Phoenix shoved her long reddish-brown hair over her shoulder. "To make your spooky Ghost, you'll first need: one empty soda bottle and a few drops of food coloring."

I sped to the equipment table with Birdie tagging right behind.

"No running," Ms. Daly called out.

My cheeks warmed. I hate getting called out. First of all, I don't like it when anyone's upset with me. Second of all, I have a little more pressure than the average student at Franklin to behave. My mom just happens to be the principal.

Believe me, it's something I can never forget.

Birdie and I wove around everyone as they grabbed what they needed off the materials table.

"No pushing," reminded Ms. Daly. "Follow our lab rules."

Birdie scooped up little bottles of red, yellow, green, and blue food coloring. "I can make purple and other colors," she cried enthusiastically as I snagged an empty plastic soda bottle.

Together, we speed-walked back to Phoenix.

"What's next?" I asked, trying to keep my impatience in check. Only I couldn't help bobbing up and down in excitement.

"You have to add water to the soda bottle," said Phoenix, reading the card extra slowly. She over-enunciated as if she were giving a speech. It irked me, but I tried not to let it show. Glancing over at the other teams, I noticed they were all reading together silently. I zipped around to glance over Phoenix's shoulder.

"Next, add the food coloring and stir," continued Phoenix. "Oh, and then add dry ice."

"I'm on it," I said. "The getting water part, that is."

At the table in front of us, Jeremy frantically

motioned to Elijah. "Hurry," shouted Jeremy and Memito at the same time. We were obviously on the very same step of the Make-a-Ghost challenge.

This wasn't good.

Elijah rushed ahead of me toward the sink. "I'm on it!"

I huffed in frustration. There was no way I could beat him without sprinting, and I wasn't about to do that again.

"Hello, I'm just walking over here," I said, smiling and waving at Ms. Daly, who stood in front of the dry ice cart. I beat Julia to the sink but was too slow to catch up to Elijah.

"Sorry, Kate. Maybe you'll beat me next time," he said, grinning. "Then again, there might not be a next time."

"Oh, there's always a next time!" I said in my most light-hearted voice. But I was feeling as rotten as a sulfuric compound. That's the stuff that makes skunks reek.

In dismay, I watched Elijah turn on the faucet full blast. As water rushed out, he hooted with happiness. Then over by Julia's table, there was a burst of cheering.

I whipped around to see that Julia wasn't in line behind me after all. Instead, she gloated as she filled up the soda bottle with the water from her insulated blue drinking bottle. Avery and Skyler clapped and whooped.

Biting my lip, I studied the speckled tile floor of the science lab. Why hadn't I thought of that?

Of course, my water bottle sat in the very bottom of my backpack, in the very back of the classroom. There was no way I could use Julia's water bottle trick to pull ahead.

"Tra la la! I don't need to go to the sink," Julia sang out, taunting me. As she shook the soda bottle, I could hear the ice clinking.

"Nice and cold!" Avery called out, while Skyler smiled in his shy way.

Wait a minute—something was off. But I couldn't quite put my finger on it.

And then, faster than a speeding electron, it came to me.

12

CHAPTER THREE

Getting Warm

Temperature (noun). Most people understand that temperature indicates hot or cold. Chemically speaking, it can help us predict which way energy flows. So when the temperature is high—like in steaming hot chocolate—there are more molecules in a state of high energy (dancing around) than there are in a cool glass of milk. Energy flow sure can be tasty!

I FIGURED OUT WHAT WAS WRONG. It all had to do with dry ice. Right when we first entered the science lab, Ms. Daly had said, "If you think a glacier is cold, then try touching dry ice. Actually don't. Never ever touch dry ice, because it's so cold it can burn you."

That meant if I wanted the chemical reaction to

work quickly and make the best Ghost, one that would hit the finish line, we would need to use *warm* water. It would turn the dry ice into a gas way faster.

I flipped on the faucet and water gushed out. It was sooooo cold.

Then I waited.

I waved my fingers through the stream, but it was still cold.

"What's taking you so long?" cried Phoenix. "Jeremy's group is about to put in their dry ice. And Julia's group already did."

As Ms. Daly pushed the cart with the tub of dry ice over to Jeremy's table, the wheels rumbled over the floor. With her silver tongs, she plopped in the pellets of dry ice.

Meanwhile, I tested the water again.

Still lukewarm. What was wrong with the pipes at this school?

"What are you doing?" cried out Phoenix. Birdie's eyebrows arched in concern.

"I'll explain later," I mumbled.

"We can't wait." Phoenix's mouth gaped open as she frantically pointed to the other groups. "Look at them!" I tried not to let the hiss of bubbles in the other bottles bother me.

Jeremy, Elijah, and Memito hunched over their bottle, screaming, "Boooooooooo!" Waving their arms, they were glowing and grinning like jack-o'-lanterns.

Meanwhile Julia, Avery, and Skyler stared in wide-eyed wonder at their experiment.

Everyone was getting ahead. But I couldn't let that stop us. "Don't worry!" I called out. "We can catch up."

Finally, at long last, the water gushed out warm. I filled the bottle up halfway, had Birdie add in the food coloring, and then speed-walked over to the cart.

I smiled up at Ms. Daly. "Ten pieces of dry ice please," I said. But not in that fake innocent way that Jeremy uses. Just in my regular voice.

"You got it, Kate," Ms. Daly said, dropping the dry ice into my bottle. It landed in the bottle with a satisfying *plunk, plunk, plunk.*

I speed-walked back to our table.

"Look!" I cried. "Bubbles are scooting to the surface." The bottle of bluish, purplish water filled with bubbles, first at the bottom, then shooting up to escape to the top.

Jumping up and down, I could feel my own bubbles of happiness.

"The pressure is building." I rubbed my hands together. "This is good. Very good!"

Shapeless curls of white vapor spurted into the air.

"Wow! It looks like a ghost," gushed Birdie. "Like the one my aunty in Ann Arbor saw in her house."

"Oh, c'mon," I said. "She was only trying to scare you."

"Nope, it was real," insisted Birdie.

"No way," I said.

"I bet she could feel the presence of the ghost right in her bones," said Phoenix. "That's how you know a ghost has shown up."

"Well, this ghost is definitely here! Look!" The Ghost rose up from the bubbling brew. It reached out a spooky, misty finger. A curl of vapor touched the yellow finish line.

"We finished the first challenge!"

hooted Phoenix, who then spun around in her ballet-like, vegan leather shoes. Her long hair swirled around her shoulders.

Birdie gawked at the shifting shape of the mist. "It's so pretty."

"Yes, it's beautiful. We did it!" I said.

Operation Ghost was a success. We all high-fived.

And that's when I heard a familiar moan, and it was coming from the corner of the room.

CHAPTER FOUR

THE ICE AGE

Dry Ice (noun). It's carbon dioxide in the solid form.
And it's super cool. Literally. As in −78° C, which is −109° F! And
when it heats up, it doesn't melt like regular water ice. Instead, it
converts directly into a gas without ever being a liquid! Some say
the gas looks like a spooky but hopefully friendly ghost.

ELIJAH BENT OVER, STARING AT HIS BOTTLE. "Hey, guys. C'mon. I'm sure it will start to explode like a volcano. Just give it a sec."

"More like eternity." Jeremy stood with his arms crossed, glaring. The reddish-orange mixture bubbled, but only a little bit. Hardly any vapor escaped.

Memito blew out an exasperated sigh. "It's never going to work, guys. We're going to lose." He slumped back in his chair. "We need a miracle."

"I bet there's a simple solution," said Elijah in an upbeat voice. But I knew he was feeling down. I watched him tug on his afro. He only did that when he was really upset. I felt awful for him.

"Check the water," I whispered from across the room.

He kept on staring at the water with hopeful eyes, like it would start to fizz as fast as opening a soda can. But that only happens because the pressure is released, and then carbon dioxide bubbles out.

"It's not a ghost. It's like a wimpy version of Alka-Seltzer," said Memito.

Elijah leaned his hands against the table. "We just need to give it more time."

"Psst, Elijah," I said, creeping toward him. "Check the water."

His brows drew together. "The water?"

"What are you doing, Kate?" asked Phoenix, frantically waving the index card for our next challenge. "We need to get started on Moon Rocks."

I held up my hand. "Hold up."

Cupping my mouth, I whispered to Elijah. "You need warmer water."

"Oh, thanks, Kate!" His lips pulled into a wide smile. "So I just need to add warm water. Will do!"

"We're supposed to use warm water?" gasped Julia, whose table was right in front of Elijah's.

"Um, yeah," I admitted a little reluctantly.

Julia frowned at her group's attempt at a Ghost. "We put in ice water." She hoisted up her water bottle. "And it's not doing anything."

"There's no mist," said Avery. "Nothing's happening."

"Just a few tiny bubbles," murmured Skyler.

"Guess we're all doomed to get bad grades," said Memito in a gloomy voice.

"Except for Kate the Chemist, Phoenix, and Birdie," said Jeremy.

"Everyone calm down." Ms. Daly made a stopping motion. "In science, if you don't like how it's going, it's fine to start again. Get new bottles and I'll take yours." Elijah and Julia eagerly handed theirs back to Ms. Daly, then they hustled over to the materials table to grab new bottles.

I strolled triumphantly back to my teammates. Only, instead of smiling, Phoenix glared at me.

"You helped Jeremy's group," she accused with a baffled expression. "And Julia's, too."

"Well, that second part was by accident. But Elijah's my friend," I said, resenting that I even needed to explain this.

Birdie shot me an understanding look. Elijah was her friend too. But since Elijah was my next-door neighbor, I've known him even longer than Birdie. He and I started hanging out when we were still in diapers. Our moms would take us to the play-ground together. I met Birdie a few years later in first grade, and we've bonded like hydrogen and oxygen in water ever since.

"Well, we'd better get started on Moon Rocks," Phoenix said. "We need to keep our lead."

"Don't worry, we've got it under control," I said. "It's all going to work out."

Uh, not really. That was the worst prediction I've ever made.

Because what happened next was the opposite of working out.

It was a science disaster of epic proportions.

CHAPTER FIVE

A SOUR MOMENT

Acid (noun). An acid is a substance that can donate a proton to another substance. That means that acids are generous. It's funny to think of lemon juice and vinegar as generous though!

A MOON ROCK IS MADE UP OF two teaspoons of water, a cup of baking soda, and a few drops of food coloring. Wearing gloves, you shape it into an alien-looking rock. Then you pour lemon juice onto the rock to watch the reaction.

Sounds simple, right?

It would be . . . if your best friend weren't an artist.

It would be . . . if she weren't obsessed with the Moon Rock becoming the perfect shade of teal blue.

"That's awesome, Birdie," I said encouragingly, as she kept on adding a little more food coloring.

"It's getting close," she admitted, biting her lip. "But I don't have the blue to yellow ratio right."

"But you do," I insisted. "Don't you think so, Phoenix?" I nudged her shoulder.

"Actually," Phoenix answered in her slow way. "It looks really close to me."

"Not quite," said Birdie. "It's too dark, almost royal blue."

"Good enough for royalty, good enough for me," I quipped. "So while you work on that, I'm going to cut up the lemon, so we can have the—" I stopped speaking.

Instead I was staring at Jeremy's group as they squeezed not one but two lemons over their misshapen green moon rock. They were pulling way ahead of us. Their group would be the ones to get to do the Vomiting Pumpkin demo, and not ours.

Memito tossed away the squeezed lemon halves while Elijah whooped in delight. "Dude, look! That's alien activity if I ever saw it."

"They're communicating with us," said Memito. "They're preparing an invasion." He cowered in mock fear.

"Nah. They're telling the mother ship that we're going to win," sang out Jeremy.

Memito puffed out his cheeks and made spluttering radio signal sounds. That kid loved to make sound effects.

"Earth to mother ship," called out Elijah. "We have conquered!"

"Not so fast!" I chopped my lemon in half super fast and raced to my table. "Okay," I said. "I'm ready with the lemons."

But I couldn't squeeze the lemons yet since Birdie was now adding silver glitter. "Don't you think it already looks great?" I said, gritting my teeth.

"And now it will look even better," gushed Birdie.

Then the rest of what she was saying was drowned out by a squealing Avery. "See! It's a crater," she cried, waving at Skyler and Julia. "We did it. It's foaming!"

They all clapped, admiring their perfect fizzy Moon Rock.

Oh, no. Suddenly, I wanted a rewind. In chemistry, they call that a *reversible reaction*. But right now, it seemed like my fate was sealed. It was irreversible. We were losing.

"Time for the final challenge!" called out Jeremy, as Elijah read the directions for the Neon Brains.

"We're behind," I said with lemon juice dripping down my arm. "So let's go!"

Birdie whirled around, holding the little bottles of food coloring. She glanced at the teal color of the rock. "It's really the perfect shade of blue now."

"Uh-huh," I said, squeezing the lemon juice over the Moon Rock. It foamed, making a crackly sound. "It worked! You guys, we can catch up," I said, trying to stay positive. "Let's just get the materials for the Neon Brains. All of them."

For the first time, Phoenix read quickly. "One tall cup, one tablespoon of dish soap, one cup of water, one highlighter, one pair of pliers, and a baking sheet."

As Birdie and I headed to the supply table, I heard Phoenix ask Ms. Daly if there could be more than one winning team. "What if there's a tie because we're all marvelous?" she asked. "And doing good things?"

"I have no problem with that possibility," said Ms. Daly, heading back to her desk.

That's when I saw Jeremy shake his head as he made his way to the supply table. "There's only going to be one winning team," he said.

Phoenix spread out her arms. "Well, if that's true, you're looking at a member of the winning team."

"That's what you think. You're such a teacher's pet," snapped Jeremy.

"Don't call her that," I growled, stepping up to Jeremy until we practically bumped noses. He was really getting on my nerves.

"*We're all so marvelous,*" said Jeremy, imitating the way Phoenix overenunciated words.

"Uh-oh," said Memito, making explosion sounds with his mouth. "There's about to be fireworks."

Elijah threw up his hands. "Don't look at me."

"Actually, she's looking at me," said Jeremy.

I jabbed my finger in the air. "Well, your team took the plastic bottle, even before we were supposed to start."

"Yeah, but we put it back," said Jeremy.

"Only because Ms. Daly told you to," hissed Phoenix.

"You guys should be disqualified!" I said.

"Wrong!" yelled Jeremy, grabbing the pliers from the supply table at the same time as me. "Let go, Kate."

"No, it's ours."

We tugged on the pliers.

Elijah stepped away from us, banging into Phoenix. With a yelp, she dropped a cup of soapy water, which thunked onto the floor and then she stepped back into the potted cactus. Her hand slid right into some needles. "Ouch!" she groaned as she swiped her hand away.

The pliers thudded onto the floor.

Ms. Daly rushed to Phoenix. "Are you all right?"

Phoenix squinted as if holding back tears. "Yes," she said, balling up her hand.

"It's all because of Jeremy!" I said.

"Well, and Elijah, too," said Phoenix.

"It was an accident!" protested Elijah.

"I hope so," said Phoenix, not looking convinced.

Then Jeremy called out, "Phoenix is a teacher's pet. And Kate and Birdie!"

Birdie folded her arms across her chest. "We are not!"

That's when Ms. Daly said in an eerily calm voice, "Everyone needs to stop talking right now." She squinted at the six of us. "I think you all know what this means."

CHAPTER SIX

BROKEN

Decomposition (noun). This means the breakdown of a molecule or a substance. It can happen when we add too much heat to a chemical. It's like breaking a chocolate chip cookie in half so now there's two crumbly pieces, instead of one whole big cookie. Of course, it's always better to eat a whole cookie!

FIRST OF ALL, YOU MUST KNOW THAT I, Kate Crawford, didn't win today's Science Challenge.

Julia's group did. They would be the ones getting to demonstrate the Vomiting Pumpkin at the Fall Festival on Friday.

But that wasn't the worst part.

The worst part was the way that Ms. Daly looked at me.

"I'm very disappointed in all of you," she said. But

her eyes zeroed in on me first. After all, I am the president of the chemistry club, so I'm supposed to be extra responsible.

It's not like I don't know the rules. You never allow yourself to get out of control in a lab. And you definitely can't get involved in a tug-of-war involving pliers when there's a potted cactus nearby. Even if Jeremy was so wrong. And extremely annoying.

During the rest of the period, Julia, Avery, and Skyler had fun with Neon Brains. Meanwhile, the rest of us sat with our heads on the table, writing all the things we did wrong in our notebooks. Right now, it felt like everything was breaking apart. In chemistry, they call that decomposition. It's when a molecule or substance breaks down. Like when you break apart hydrogen peroxide, for example. The chemical bonds are broken in the peroxide, and then you end up with oxygen gas and liquid water—two separate things.

Depending on what's happening, decomposition can happen all at once or in a series of steps.

"I'm afraid you six will all receive zeroes for today," said Ms. Daly.

I swallowed hard. Right now, I felt like my life was

decomposing all at once! Birdie had tears in her eyes. Phoenix pulled on her macramé bracelet.

Elijah stared at the wall, and Jeremy pointed at me, smirking.

Memito jutted out his lower lip, sighing heavily.

With furrowed brows, Ms. Daly said in a scary, quiet voice. "And I'd like to see all six of you after school tomorrow. It's important that you be there."

My head felt so heavy I thought it might roll right off my neck.

This wasn't all my fault. Was it?

CHAPTER SEVEN

A GALAXY OF DISAPPOINTMENT

Scientific Fact (noun). A simple observation of the world that does not change over time. Unlike fashion, which changes all of the time. And, of course, the weather.

NOTHING WAS GOING RIGHT. During lunch, I sat at the end of a long table with Birdie, Phoenix, and Avery. Nobody was speaking. I stared at my  bologna sandwich. Ugh. Bologna. Ham is my favorite lunchmeat. It's square, my favorite shape, because I like defined edges and corners. The circular bologna was covered with a piece of crisp lettuce. I could only take one bite and then stared at an unopened bag of potato chips.

To make things worse, Fall Festival posters lined every wall of the cafeteria. "I can't believe we're not going to be able to do the Vomiting Pumpkin demo at the festival," I said, closing my eyes so I didn't have to be tortured by the sight of the posters featuring grinning jack-o'-lanterns.

"The festival will still be fun," said Birdie. "Face painting, caramel apples."

"Bean bag toss, the cakewalk, and the costume photo booth," said Phoenix.

"Sack races, the bouncy houses, fun cheesy prizes," added Avery.

"I just can't get happy about it," I admitted. "It's because of the"—I could barely say the word—"the detention."

After opening her stainless-steel container, Phoenix dipped a stick of celery into the hummus inside. "I didn't know that detentions were a thing at our school," she said.

"They're not." I could hardly swallow.

"I guess you would know," said Avery. "Since your mom is the principal."

"Thanks for pointing that out," I mumbled. Sometimes Avery knew how to poke a sore spot. I mean, of course I knew that my mom was the principal. I've only lived with her for all ten years of my life. And of course I was freaked out about having to report after school tomorrow for what appeared to be a detention. Did she really need to rub it in? Already I was regretting eating with Avery. But when you decide to eat with Phoenix, it also means eating with Avery. They're bonded like atoms in a molecule.

Phoenix crunched on a celery stick. Birdie started to doodle in her notebook. Well, not really doodle—she was furiously drawing spirals. She whispered, "Do you think your mom will be really mad, Kate?"

I sagged into my chair. "I don't even want to think about it." Not only would my parents be unhappy, but I was truly disappointed in myself. A whole galaxy of disappointment.

Normally, Elijah eats with us too, but today he was eating with Jeremy and Memito at the far end of our long rectangular table. Honestly, I was surprised that they weren't sitting at the opposite end of the cafeteria. Or the universe.

"I heard detentions go on your permanent record," called out Memito, twirling the lid of his thermos on his finger. "Then in middle school you get labeled as a troublemaker. And it follows you to high school, too."

"That's not true," I said. "It would have to be way more serious for that to happen." Nearby, one of the monitors, Ms. Giosso, was directing kids to throw away their recycling in the proper bin. For a moment, her eyes scanned our table. Suddenly I wondered if she had heard about our detention.

"Staying after school is not good," said Elijah, staring glumly at his applesauce.

"Yeah, it's not awesome," agreed Jeremy, although he didn't look all that sad. "But it's not the biggest deal."

"I think it's a big deal." Memito made a farting sound by sticking out his tongue. Elijah laughed.

"Eh." Jeremy shrugged. "It'll be just another afternoon at Franklin Elementary."

"I don't think so," said Phoenix, waving her hand, which had a Band-Aid where the cactus needles had pricked her palm.

"Mmm, these fries are tasty," said Jeremy, dipping a french fry in some ketchup. Leaning back, he tipped his chair like it was a rocker. Jeremy hardly seemed disturbed, which wasn't like him.

"How can you be happy?" Just as the lunch monitor stepped closer to our table, Phoenix flung a crumpled napkin over at Jeremy.

Ms. Giosso marched right up to our table. I braced myself. Phoenix was about to be written up. The monitor stopped at the head of the table. Her eyes locked with Phoenix's. "Did I just see you throw a napkin?" she asked.

"Yes, you did!" said Phoenix, pronouncing each word like she was on stage. She smiled proudly. "I just learned how to throw a curveball. And I was practicing a two-seam grip. My cousin's on the softball team at Sonoma State, in California, and showed me via Skype."

"Really?" Ms. Giosso patted her throat. "I played softball in high school. You're looking at the shortstop." She glanced at the glass wall overlooking the playing field. "Next time, practice that curveball out there. Okay?"

"Oh yes, will do," said Phoenix as Ms. Giosso headed over to the salad bar, where some kids were tossing tongs.

Memito pretended to mop his brow. "Phew," he said. "That was too close."

Jeremy rolled his eyes. "If that had been me, I would have gotten a detention on the spot."

"Please don't say that word," I begged. *"Detention."*

"Kate, don't worry," said Elijah. "Maybe it's not an actual detention. Maybe it's just a special chemistry club meeting."

"Good try," I said. "Except chemistry club was canceled this week because of the Science Challenge."

"I don't think it could be anything else but a detention," groaned Memito.

"Let's get real," said Jeremy. "Ms. Daly is kind of old. And back in the olden times, they did stuff like that."

"Ageism!" accused Phoenix, wagging her finger as Jeremy made a face. "That's prejudice against older people. Girls, I'm thinking we should sit at a different table."

"Yeah," I said.

"Agreed," said Birdie.

Then the bell rang.

And it was too late.

"Well, you can try to avoid us,

Phoenix," said Jeremy. "But we'll be seeing all of you at your doomsday tomorrow afternoon." He threw back his head, smirking. "Bye-bye!" he said getting up to go with Elijah and Memito.

"Hey! It's your doomsday too," I said.

Jeremy gave us a thumbs-up, then disappeared along with Elijah and Memito into the crowd leaving the cafeteria.

Popping off my seat, I turned to Phoenix and Birdie. "There's something going on with him. I don't know what it is. But I'm going to figure it out."

CHAPTER EIGHT

COLLIDING ON AND OFF THE FIELD

Collision Theory (noun). When two molecules collide, they transfer kinetic energy, which can break bonds within the molecules. But this is a good thing, because it means that new bonds can be made. Think of it like playing Red Rover, where a kid crashes through linked hands. But then different hands can link, and the fun game can continue.

"OKAY, THIS IS REALLY THE LAST STRAW," said Phoenix, grimacing as she punched the tetherball super hard.

I was about to punch it back but I caught the ball instead. "Wasn't that your bad hand?" I said.

Phoenix gazed down in surprise. "I definitely shouldn't have done that. I can still feel those cactus needles." She turned and gazed over at Birdie. "I think I'm going to sit down." Phoenix never sits down during recess so I knew she must still be in a little bit of pain. Avery, on the other hand, often sat inside during recess to read.

Phoenix plopped down next to Birdie, who was sketching at a nearby picnic table. I went over to join them and inspected Birdie's drawing. It was a creepy vampire with streaks of purple in his blond hair. Only this vampire wasn't sleeping in a crypt, but on a giant soccer ball. And he looked really familiar.

"That's Jeremy," I said.

"You definitely captured his personality," said Phoenix.

I gazed at the blue October sky. Canada geese flew overhead in a V formation. It was warm enough that we didn't need our coats, just sweaters. "I really want to find out why Jeremy's not more bothered by the detention. It's so strange."

I hopped off the picnic bench. "Let's go over by the field."

"You think watching him play soccer is going to help?" asked Phoenix.

"Well, we won't learn anything just sitting here," I

said. We were like a bunch of molecules in a solid, hardly moving. Just sort of vibrating.

"I'm in." Birdie snapped shut her sketchbook.

"Me too," said Phoenix. "Most definitely."

We crept closer to the field and settled in by some mulberry bushes, close enough so we could eavesdrop.

"Memito, your shoes are untied," said Jeremy just after he finished scoring a goal.

"You'll trip," warned Elijah.

Memito adjusted his baseball cap. "Maybe I'll break my right arm. And then I'll get an excuse for the rest of the month. I won't be able to do any writing."

"They'll make you write with your left hand," said Jeremy.

"That would be scary," said Memito, kicking up some grass. "I'd write like a preschooler. No, way worse. An alien."

"I'd write for you," offered Elijah.

"Dude, no. You've got such bad handwriting," said Memito. "And your hands are sticky."

"*My* hands?" said Elijah. "You're the one always eating power bars."

"That why I'm full of power." Memito raised both of his arms in a champion salute.

They weren't talking about real stuff, just stuff like a broken arm that might possibly happen. In science, that's not even a hypothesis, because a hypothesis is stuff that you expect to be true.

With a sigh, I signaled for us to head back to the picnic table. We were just about to leave when Elijah stepped up to us.

"Hey," he said. "What are you all doing?"

"Nothing," said Phoenix.

"Yeah," added Birdie.

"Bird watching." I giggled, pointing to Birdie.

"Ha ha." Elijah didn't look convinced though. "Hey, Kate, do you think that your mom can take me home tomorrow? After our detention."

I didn't say anything. Right now, I was annoyed at Elijah. How could he be hanging around with Jeremy?

"Did you hear what I just said?" he said.

"Yeah"

"So?"

I shrugged. "I guess my mom can drive you." Suddenly, it reminded me all over again of the upcoming detention. Today wasn't going so well. And the forecast for tomorrow wasn't looking any better.

secrets to keep

Metabolism (noun). A chemical process that happens in cells and organisms to convert food into energy. Or how your body converts that hot dog you ate into a cartwheel.

AFTER SCHOOL, I GRABBED A chocolate chip granola bar that I hadn't eaten during lunch from my backpack. Plopping down in a chair, I considered when the best time would be to tell my parents about what happened during the Science Challenge.

There didn't seem to be a good time.

But it was a good time for getting some energy out. I guess you could say I was ready for an exothermic reaction. In chemistry, that's when energy is released into an environment. So I headed to the backyard to kick a soccer ball against a wooden practice wall that my dad had built for me, where I definitely released a whole bunch of energy.

After that, I tried doing my math homework on the kitchen table. Only we had to answer questions about the role of base numbers versus exponents. Like we had to explain 7^2 meant the same as 7 x 7. And that 7 was the base number and 2 was the exponent. Why couldn't we just have regular math homework? I would really love some busywork right now.

As I stared at the blank page in my workbook, a delicious aroma filled the kitchen. On the oven top, a whole chicken and a bunch of roasted vegetables were cooling. It looked like Dad had gotten everything ready for dinner, except for setting the table, which was my job.

My dog, Dribble, trotted to the oven. "Smells good, right?" I said. "It's not for you, silly. It's human food."

His fluffy rust-colored tail wagged back and forth. I really shouldn't have said that word. *Food.* When we first adopted him last year from the animal shelter, he had the biggest appetite. And nothing's changed. He always thinks it's dinnertime. Dribble nosed over to me, and I scratched him behind the ears.

43

I felt so guilty about even mentioning food, I plopped a handful of dog treats into his bowl. "This is your pre-dinner snack," I told him.

My feeling of guilt didn't lift though. Chewing on my knuckle, I thought about the Science Challenge, Jeremy, and the detention.

I should probably tell Mom and Dad the awful details after they had eaten some of their dinner. You see, nobody in my family is easygoing when they're hungry. Not even my dog. Dribble crunched his treats down in practically one swallow. He looked at me with sad and hopeful doggy eyes. I knew exactly how he felt.

I heard a chair scrape against the floor above me. Dad was in his home office going over paperwork. He's a therapist and has a ton of paperwork. That means when he's in the zone of filling out forms, I'm pretty much safe from him asking me too many questions. I glanced up at the clock on the microwave. It was already 6:15 p.m. Mom should be home any second.

Ugh.

Today, Mom had an extra-late meeting after school. I almost never get a ride home with her, because once school is over, she's usually at a meeting. But I do go

44

home with her on the days I have after-school activities, like chemistry club. Or, I guess, if I get detention.

I flopped back in my chair, and my thoughts spun. What if Mom already knew about the incident? What if Ms. Daly had already told her, and the entire staff at Rosalind Franklin Elementary was horrified that her usually pretty well-behaved, science-obsessed daughter had gotten into trouble?

Someone thudded into the kitchen. Someone not very big but very loud: my five-year-old brother, Liam.

"Want to see my Lego ship?" he asked. It was more of a command than a question.

"Sure."

He dragged me into the family room, where he had an entire fleet of Lego space-ships. "See, that's the refueling station," he said, pointing to a flat gray piece with multicolored squares on it.

"Wow."

"And that's where they get secret weapons. They're invisible."

"Uh-huh."

"You're not listening." He flopped to the floor and

folded his arms across this chest. He sounded and looked just like a miniature version of Dad. However, everyone knows Liam is my brother because we have the exact same hair color. Light brown with bright gold highlights. Liam made such a cute grumpy face that I laughed.

"Sorry," I said. "I'm tired." Tired of trying to figure out what to do next, that was.

Suddenly, Mom peeked into the family room. I hadn't even heard her car pull up the driveway. Or the click of her heels as she headed into the house.

"Are you coming down with something?" she asked, placing the back of her hand on my forehead. "You don't feel warm, Kate."

"I'm fine," I said, which wasn't exactly true.

"Are you sure?" she asked.

I nodded my head emphatically.

"Let's just keep an eye on things," she said in the quiet voice she uses when her voice is strained at the end of a long day.

After Mom changed into her comfortable clothes and I set the table, it was time to eat. And for me to face the jury, aka my parents.

Mom complimented Dad on the chicken. "You roasted it perfectly," she said. "Oh, and you made cauliflower rice. Thank you, honey. My fitness boot camp ladies will be proud."

I really wanted this meal to speed up so I could get the bad part over with.

My parents did their usual routine, asking about everyone's day.

Mom asked Dad how things went at work. Since Dad's a therapist, he can't give away details about his patients. But he can give an overview.

When Dad turned to Mom and asked about her day, she looked a little pale. "It was great," she said, though her voice sounded tired. "I think our third-grade team is really onto something special with their cross-curricular use of pumpkins for everything from math to social studies. And the Fall Festival is shaping up. But—" Mom blinked. She massaged her forehead. "I've got a headache. It started in the middle of the faculty meeting. I should have grabbed something for it. But I didn't." She winced. "I think it's getting worse. It's all the budget stuff at school coupled with the Fall Festival planning."

"The Fall Festival!" cried Liam. "Can we go! Can we?"

"Of course," said Dad, "but right now let's use our inside voice. Mom's not feeling so great."

Mom winced, almost apologetically.

I wasn't the one not feeling well. It was Mom.

Dad immediately got up to dim the lights. "Honey, I'm sorry. You should have told me." He turned to look at me and Liam. "Be right back. I'm getting your mother something." He went upstairs and returned with a couple of Tylenol. "Here you go."

Mom took the medicine and washed it down with a sip of water. "Thank you," she said with a grateful but strained smile.

"How was your day, Kate?" Dad said, turning to me. "I know Liam had a good day."

"Yeah, I build-ed six X-wing fighters," said Liam, shoveling a giant helping of cauliflower rice into his mouth.

"Built," corrected Mom softly, in her headache voice.

"Yeah, that," said Liam.

"Good," said Dad. "I'm glad you are creating a fleet. Maybe we have an aerospace engineer on our hands. As well as a chemist." Dad flicked his eyes at me. He looked proud.

"Okay, Kate. Give us your report."

So I told my family about all the best parts, only quickly mentioning the Fall Science Challenge.

"Tell us more about how the Fall Science Challenge went," said Mom. "Did it all work out okay?" She emphasized the phrase 'work out' in a weird way.

I felt uneasy as she steepled her fingers.

But no, I told myself. She was just curious. My parents are always curious about me. I felt bad that she was trying so hard to be a good mom while she wasn't feeling well.

"Yes," said Dad. "We want to hear what happened."

Only just a little bit of pressure. Great.

"I heard that Ms. Daly knocked herself out with the challenges this year," continued Mom. "But that maybe there was a little more to it than normal."

Taking a deep breath, I tried to relax. "The Science Challenge today was amazing," I said, pausing. Did Mom know? Did Dad? They certainly weren't acting like it. They both were semi-smiling.

"So what did you do?" pressed Liam. He pointed to my parents. "Terri and Greg want to know."

Mom cleared her throat in disapproval.

"Call us Mom and Dad," said Dad patiently. "Only friends should use our first names."

"And don't point," Mom added.

Uh-oh. This wasn't shaping up well. This meant I had to focus on positive things. And shift the family mood.

So I told everyone about the Ghost and the out-of-this-world Moon Rocks. And the glowy Neon Brains, even though my group didn't have a chance to do that demo.

"Gosh, Kate, I'm feeling a little bit better," said Mom, her voice noticeably lighter. "Just hearing about all of this wonderful science you're doing with Ms. Daly is easing my headache."

"I'm glad," said Dad.

"Me too," I said. "There's something I want to tell you."

"Oh really?" asked Dad, giving Mom a look.

"Looks like I'll need a ride from you tomorrow," I blurted out. Suddenly, it didn't seem like a good idea to tell them about what had happened. Not when Mom's headache was just starting to get better. Even Dribble stood nearby wagging his tail, happy that he had finally been fed.

Things were better! I couldn't be the one to ruin them.

"But I thought chemistry club was canceled," said Mom, her forehead wrinkling in confusion.

"Ah, kind of. Ms. Daly just wanted a bunch of us to sort of stay after school."

"Oh, sounds like she has something interesting in store for you," Dad said, nodding as if that made perfect sense.

My stomach knotted.

"When you put your mind to it, you can be such a good helper," Mom said, smiling at me.

I just sat there staring at my cauliflower rice and chicken. Actually, *I* was the one who was a chicken. I was pretty surprised I didn't start clucking. And then I thought about how cauliflower isn't rice at all. Instead, it's pieces of cauliflower that have been cut up to look like rice.

It's fake. Just like me.

CHAPTER TEN

DETENTION

Scientific Paper (noun). This is a written report that explains the research a scientist has completed. A report usually consists of an introduction, an experimental section, a results and discussion section, and, most important, a conclusion. Just like with any good movie, you need to see how it ends! Scientists always want to read a good conclusion.

ON WEDNESDAY AFTERNOON, Birdie and I shuffled down the hallway toward the science lab. Today was tough, even though we had our drumming class. (Elijah was in heaven.) All I could think about was our detention. And now it was happening.

We passed a giant banner that read: BUY YOUR FALL FESTIVAL WRISTBANDS IN ADVANCE! Right now, I didn't want to think about anything in advance, especially not what was coming next. Phoenix strode ahead. The back of her vintage rainbow shirt made the world seem happy, even though it wasn't right now.

Normally, moving slowly is not my thing. But I wanted to avoid the inevitable.

My first and hopefully last detention.

Just as we passed the central office, Phoenix disappeared around the corner.

And at that very moment, none other than my mother, the principal of Rosalind Franklin Elementary, hurried out of the main office doorway, which says ALL VISITORS TO FRANKLIN ELEMENTARY MUST SIGN IN.

My stomach dropped to the school's foundation.

"Hi, girls," my mom said in her usual nonheadachy, cheerful voice. She clutched a lined yellow notepad in her arms. Even though it was after a full day, her brown suit looked as crisp as it had this morning.

"I can see you're off to chemistry club," she said. "Just swing on by when you all are ready to go home."

"Sure," I said in what I hoped was a peppy voice.

I gave Birdie a *please-don't-say-anything* look. But Birdie didn't glance back. For some reason, she studied the floor like she might trip on her shoelaces.

We speed-walked away from the office. "You didn't

tell her?" whispered Birdie, still studying her sneakers.

"No," I admitted.

"I guess you must be pretty upset not to tell your mom. You tell her *everything*."

"Yeah." My voice caught. Birdie knows I always give my family a summary of my day at dinner. My dad jokingly calls it my scientific report.

"Did you tell your parents?" I asked Birdie.

"Yes. Kind of. And my mom immediately wanted to call up Jeremy's mom, and, well, your mom. But I talked her out of it."

"That's good news." Birdie's mom is a lawyer, and when she gets worked up about something, you know it. When she goes to court, she has to convince people that her client is correct. She fights really hard for them by outlining all the evidence that supports her argument. Birdie and I once got to watch her practice what she was going to say. And wow.

"It's odd that Ms. Daly didn't at least tell your mom what happened," said Birdie.

"Yeah." I shrugged. "I have no clue why."

We ducked into the science lab and went to the table, where Phoenix was already sitting down. Nearby on the materials table was a bag of iron oxide powder and a bottle of distilled water. Also, in the back of the lab sat stacks of cardboard boxes. Normally, I'd be curious about what we might do with them. But not today.

I just wanted to get this over with. I also wanted Birdie to tell me what was bothering her—if it was just science detention or something else. But I wasn't about to ask her about it in front of other people. What if I was the reason she looked so upset? I thought about how impatient I had been yesterday. Oh, gosh. It probably was because of me.

Ms. Daly sat at her desk, reading over some papers. She didn't even glance up. She didn't even say hello.

This wasn't a good start.

Elijah moped at the table across from us and barely waved hello. Memito and Jeremy swung into the room and plopped down. Memito glanced at the clock on the wall as if he was willing it to say 4:00 p.m.

I got that.

But not Jeremy. He grinned so hard his dimples

pressed into his cheeks. He folded his hands in his lap and sat up extra straight. "We're ready for our detention," he said in an enthusiastic voice.

Ms. Daly pressed her hands into the desk. "Detention? What gave you the idea that this is a detention?"

"Because it's after school," said Jeremy almost giddily. "And you're really angry with us, right?"

"Angry?" Ms. Daly shook her head so fast you could just see a blur of silver hair. "Ooooh, you kids would know if I was upset." She popped out of her chair and paced in front of her desk. "You messed up, but I believe in all sorts of proactive interventions and that's why you're here today. This isn't a detention."

"Aw, man." Jeremy slumped back in his chair and huffed.

I swiveled around, trying to understand how Jeremy could possibly be disappointed.

"Jeremy, you're not even making a teensy weensy"—Memito held up his fingers like he was pinching them—"bit of sense."

"My thoughts exactly," I said.

"Dude, you actually want a detention?" Elijah shook his head. "Are you dehydrated or something?"

56

Ms. Daly motioned for us all to stop talking. "Let's review some important rules that you didn't follow yesterday."

She grabbed a neon-yellow metric ruler and tapped the Science Lab Rules poster, which hung right above her desk. "Be responsible at all times. No horseplay, practical jokes, or pranks."

"Horseplay sounds way dangerous," said Memito. "Like you're playing with a horse in school. Those things kick."

"Or it's a theater show about a horse," said Elijah. And Memito neighed.

"I don't think so," said Phoenix, rolling her eyes.

"They're joking," said Jeremy with a cool shrug. "Can't you people take a joke?"

"Not in a science lab," said Birdie, pointing up at the poster of rules.

Phoenix raised her hand. "Exactly, because horseplay means you're goofing off."

"That's a word my grandpa uses," said Jeremy. "It's weird."

"Well, you can't horseplay here," said Ms. Daly. "Whether it's a weird word or not. And this rule is very important." She once again gestured up at the list of rules. "Handle all science materials and tools carefully. And put things back."

I raised my hand. "I guess that means no tug-of-war."

"Bingo!" shouted Ms. Daly. "Give that girl some protective lab goggles, because her life is going to be so bright." She rocked forward and knit her hands together. "I think you all are very clear on why I'm disappointed in my best students. And why you all won't be participating in the final fifth-grade Science Challenge on Thursday." She paused. "An escape room."

Loud groans filled the science lab.

"What?" said Elijah, smacking his hands on the table like a final drum roll. "An escape room? Are you serious? The entire fifth grade is going to do an escape room and we can't?"

"My cousin in Kansas said it could be your dream— or your nightmare," moaned Memito in mock horror. "They lock you up and throw away the key. It's like prison. If you're not smart enough to get out, that is."

"Well, I'm plenty smart, so that wouldn't happen to me," said Jeremy, jabbing his pencil in the air for emphasis.

All I could think about was how much I've wanted to go to an escape room. For a really long time. At least for the past six months. Ever since Memito's cousin told him about it, and Memito told Birdie and me. It just seems so cool to see if you can solve the mystery and beat the clock. "So it's a field trip that everyone gets to go on *except us*?" I asked.

Ms. Daly waved her arms. "Whoa. First of all, nobody is going anywhere. The escape room is here in the school. That's what all of the boxes are for." She gestured to the back of the room at the stacks of cardboard boxes. "I've been secretly working on it for the last six weeks. It's all set up in the PTA office. Which you probably know is just three rooms down from us."

"The PTA office has been turned into an escape room?" I said. "That's so cool!"

"Not for us," said Jeremy. "We can't go."

"Did I say no to the escape room?" Ms. Daly gestured with her arms like she was holding a tray. "I didn't. I said that you wouldn't be going to the escape room along with the other fifth graders. Instead you have a chance to test it out right now—if you all agree to work together."

"We have to work with them?" gasped Phoenix, nodding at the boys.

"We're going to be stuck with the girls?" Jeremy's face puckered. I could hear Memito softly groan.

"Yup, exactly," Ms. Daly said. "It's all about teamwork. And if you can work together, then those big fat zeroes you got in lab will"—she swiped the air—"magically go away. This is your choice. However, if one of you doesn't want to do it, then nobody will be able to do it." She leaned forward, scanning our faces. "So what do you want to do?"

"I'm so in!" I said, relief ballooning inside of me.

"Me too," said Birdie, who for the first time was acting a little more normal.

"It's definitely better than study hall or detention or staring at each other in silence," said Memito. "That'd be *so* boring that you might fall asleep and could get science nightmares."

"Ha ha," I said.

"Guys, I think we should do it," said Elijah. "I'm down."

"I'm not," said Jeremy. "I don't want to do it with the girls." His eyes zeroed in on Phoenix.

"And I don't want to do it if *he's* doing it," said Phoenix, shaking her head. "Plus, I'm not a fan of anything timed."

"Just forget about the clock," I said, trying to keep positive. "It'll be really fun."

"Dude, Jeremy. C'mon, you've got to say yes," said Elijah, clutching Jeremy's shoulder. "Because of what happened, my mom won't let me play the drums for a week. I can't go more than a day without my beats."

"Okay, folks, I need to know now," said Ms. Daly. "So what's it going to be?"

"Well," said Jeremy. "I've made up my mind."

"Me too," said Phoenix.

CHAPTER ELEVEN

THE SURVIVAL INSTRUCTIONS

Deoxyribonucleic Acid (noun). DNA contains instructions that tell living things how to develop and function. It's like a secret code that is unique to each person. Detectives can even use DNA left at crime scenes to catch the bad guys!

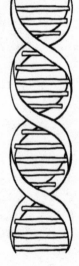

"AND THE ANSWER IS?" I prompted. "Will you please say yes to doing the escape room?"

"Okay." Jeremy gave a thumbs-up. "Since Elijah asked. And I guess it's actually cool that we're doing this."

Phoenix waved her bandaged hand. "If everyone else really wants to do it, then I'm in."

"Yes!" I said. "Yes, oh yes!"

"Good. I thought you'd see the light," said Ms. Daly.

"My older brother's going to be so jealous," said Jeremy, his voice actually sounding a little enthusiastic.

Birdie fidgeted with her pen and sighed. What was up with her?

"Um, I just have one question," said Phoenix. "What's an escape room?"

"What?" Jeremy dramatically slapped his forehead. "Dude, have you been living under a rock or something?"

"Don't call me dude," said Phoenix in her slow, calm voice. "And no. My family doesn't own a TV. By choice. And we don't live under a rock, although our house is at the bottom of a slight rocky incline."

"We don't need any more fighting around here," said Ms. Daly. "As soon as I explain more about the escape room, we'll be all set. And luckily all of your parents have already signed the waiver forms electronically."

Okay, my mind was just blown. This meant that Mom and Dad knew the entire time?

"Waiver forms?" Jeremy leaned forward. "That's, like, when you do something dangerous. Now I'm extra into this."

Me too. I couldn't wait to get started. Suddenly, the worst afternoon of my life wasn't looking so bad. "I can't believe we get to do an escape room." *Even if it's with Jeremy and his bad attitude.*

"How many of you have done an escape room before?" asked Ms. Daly.

Birdie raised her hand. "Me."

"You have?" I said. Usually I knew if Birdie had done anything cool.

"Yeah." Birdie clenched her fist. I really didn't get why she was acting so strange. "It was for my sister's birthday. My mom ordered a kit."

"That doesn't count," said Jeremy.

"Why not?" I said, defending my BFF.

"Listen, everyone, let's remain calm," said Ms. Daly. "Because you're going to need to cooperate if you plan on getting out of the escape room." She looked around ominously.

"Is it scary?" I asked in a casual voice. But I didn't feel casual. Instead, I felt a little scared, if you want to know the truth. While I love science and puzzles, I'm definitely not the kind of person who's into spooky stuff like actual ghosts or anything creepy.

"Let's just say it's a very exciting, high-stakes experience," stated Ms. Daly. "And it involves a famous scientist whose research led to the understanding of DNA, as in the building block of all life."

"Yes!" I couldn't help popping out of my seat. "I know who it might be."

"Shh." Ms. Daly placed her fingers on her lips. "Hold your horses, Kate. All right, folks, I'll give you your instructions, but first off, give me your phones. And put away your backpacks." She pointed to the cubbies on the side wall.

Everyone handed over their phones, and Ms. Daly placed them in a plastic blue tub. Then we stuffed our backpacks into the cubbies.

Ms. Daly glanced behind her as if someone might be listening in on our conversation. She then lowered her voice conspiratorially. "Okay, you're about to enter the game world. This is a game full of puzzles you must solve in order to move on to the next clue. You must be organized. And you must work together. I recommend that you look for clues and communicate with each other if you want to have any chance of getting out of the escape room in time."

Ms. Daly's face grew even more serious. "Handle everything with great care," she continued. "Do not move anything that doesn't move easily. Do not take anything apart. If it's a real clue, you can remove it easily. There are multiple cameras set up in the room, so I will be monitoring you the entire time. If anyone feels that they need to leave, you just call out my name. But if you leave, that will be the end of the game and you will have lost. Oh, and no eating in the room."

Everyone looked at Memito. "That would mean no snacks," he moaned.

"Exactly." Ms. Daly raised her eyebrows. "Any other questions?"

"What happens if we don't get out?" asked Memito. "Like, something really bad?"

"Well, you like this school, right?" said Ms. Daly. "You'll just spend the rest of your life here, then."

Memito and Elijah gazed at each other, their mouths open. Birdie shifted uncomfortably in her seat. And honestly, I was a little worried, too.

66

"I'm joking," said Ms. Daly. "I'm just going to go behind that screen over there, and I'll be right back." She pointed to a dark brown folding screen. "While I'm away, I'd like everyone to put on your lab coats." Then she disappeared behind the screen.

I rubbed my hands together. "Oh, this sounds science-y, you guys."

Grabbing a lab coat, I pulled a pair of protective goggles around my neck just to be safe. As I was tucking a pair of gloves into my pocket, a silver-haired person with dark mirrored glasses stomped back into the room.

CHAPTER TWELVE

THE CLOCK STARTS TO TICK

Rosalind Franklin (legendary scientist). A British chemist who played a crucial role in understanding DNA. She's a science superhero who used X-rays to take images of DNA. She had so much fun that she used the X-rays to study all kinds of things, even dangerous viruses!

"JUST CALL ME BLANCHE VIPER," said the silver-haired woman in a gravelly voice. Honestly, I knew it was Ms. Daly wearing a disguise. But with the sunglasses and brown suit, she looked like a real spy. Maybe because the lights were dimmed, and moody jazz music was playing from the speakers on the desk.

It felt like we had stepped right into an old movie. Birdie sort of clutched the desk, and even Jeremy didn't attempt to crack a joke.

Blanche motioned for us to follow her into the hallway. "We must enter a time portal." She directed us past a couple of classrooms to the end of the corridor, then stopped in front of the PTA office. "We have gone back in time. It's now 1953."

"Wow, that's before Pop-Tarts," said Memito.

"Or Guitar Hero," said Elijah.

"Or YouTube," continued Jeremy.

"Yes, well, it was more than a half century ago," said Blanche. "Now come closer to me." We all edged around the spy. "I work for—well, I can't tell you the name of my organization." Blanche lowered her voice. "It's top secret. But I need your help. It's urgent. You see, Dr. Rosalind Franklin—yes, one of the world's greatest scientists—was in the middle of making a breakthrough in chemistry."

"Oh, Rosalind Franklin is my favorite scientist in all of history," I said.

"Well, she should be," cried Elijah. "She's who our school is named after."

"Shhh," said Phoenix. "We need to listen."

The spy known as Blanche Viper looked left and right as if someone might sneak up the hallway at any second. "I must be quick. You see, while working for a secret branch of the government, Central Headquarters for the Knights of Science, Dr. Franklin was using X-rays to take images of a secret, rare, and deadly virus. But our sources learned that the evil mastermind Dr. Hans Dragas plans to steal the last remaining image in her lab."

"Of the virus?" asked Memito, his eyes wide.

"Yes, it's one of the deadliest viruses that ever existed. Dr. Dragas and his associates want to use it so they can copy the virus and unleash it on the world."

Memito made a low whistle. "That's rough. Almost as bad as a zombie apocalypse."

"Isn't there some kind of antidote?" I asked.

"I'm afraid not," said the spy previously known as Ms. Daly. "Dr. Franklin disappeared two weeks ago. You must find her breakthrough image and give it to me before the evil Dr. Hans Dragas gets to her lab." She looked down at her silver wristwatch. "Which intel suggests will be in forty minutes.

"Not much time," yelped Memito.

"You are about to enter Dr. Franklin's lab," she said, pointing to the PTA office. Or rather the former PTA office. I noticed a little piece of paper taped to the door that said DR. FRANKLIN'S LAB. "Once the door closes behind you, the clock starts," continued Blanche. "Are you prepared to take on this grave responsibility? You must find Dr. Franklin's image of the virus and get out of the lab before Dr. Dragas and his henchman arrive. Which is in forty minutes. Otherwise, the virus will be unleashed upon the entire world."

"Yes, let's do it!" I cried.

"Great," said Blanche, and she handed Memito an egg timer. "So you can keep track of your time. Give yourself forty minutes as soon as you enter the lab. The main door to the lab will have a combination lock," she said. "That's the one you need to figure out how to open in order to escape. We're entering the lab by a side door. After you enter, I'm closing that side door, and you won't be able to open it back up, unless you want to forfeit."

We all shook our heads. Nobody wanted to do that.

A moment later, we shuffled into Dr. Franklin's lab. It was so dark you could barely see the person in front of you. Creepy music played in the background.

"Is this a lab or a haunted house?" asked Elijah. "Because if it's a haunted house, I know how to take care of ghosts. I watched that movie *Ghost Busters*."

I laughed out of relief. "Can we please turn on the lights?"

"Yes," said Blanche. "But it will only brighten the room a little bit." Then she closed the door behind her with a bang. When we turned on the lights, we couldn't believe what stood right in front of us.

CHAPTER THIRTEEN

A COOL SETUP

Condenser (noun). A device that chemists use in labs that looks like a goofy glass tube. It's super fancy because it is used to transform a gas to a liquid. The vapor passes through the cold tube and turns into cute little droplets. So it sort of acts like a little refrigerator.

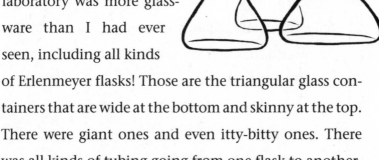

INSIDE OF DR. FRANKLIN'S laboratory was more glassware than I had ever seen, including all kinds of Erlenmeyer flasks! Those are the triangular glass containers that are wide at the bottom and skinny at the top. There were giant ones and even itty-bitty ones. There was all kinds of tubing going from one flask to another. Oh, plus dozens of test tubes. And a Bunsen burner to heat liquids and stuff.

"This is awesome," I said. "They even have con-densers." I pointed to some horizontal glass pipes that were moving chemicals from one spot to another.

"I don't see the X-ray machine that Dr. Franklin used to take images," said Phoenix.

"She probably locked it up," said Memito, turning on the egg timer to start the countdown.

"Right," said Elijah. "She didn't want that evil Dr. Dragas to get his hands on it."

Elijah pointed to the front door of the lab. It had a combination lock on it. "Somehow we're going to have to figure out the code to that thing."

"Meanwhile, check out that closet," said Birdie in a nervous voice. "It's a wreck." A bunch of lab coats were piled in a heap on the floor.

"I'm on it," said Elijah, hurrying into the closet.

"It's weird that the lab coats are on the floor," said Phoenix thoughtfully. "I read a biography of Rosalind Franklin over the summer, and it said she was always very neat and careful."

"Yes, yes, good point," I admitted. And a little teeny part of me was jealous. I should have been the one to have read the Franklin bio. After all, I'm the kid obsessed with chemistry, and Rosalind Franklin is the queen of chemistry.

Elijah stepped out of the closet, making a frowny face. "Nope, nothing in the closet. I checked everywhere. But I did put on a new lab coat. The one I had was too small."

Suddenly, Phoenix dropped down to the floor and scooped up a clue. "Got something!" she announced, waving a small, bright red journal.

"Mmm. That color reminds me of candied apples," said Memito. "Which I'm definitely getting at the Fall Festival."

"Shh," said Phoenix. "We're not going to the festival unless we can escape from here." Carefully she flipped through the pages. "It's Dr. Franklin's diary," she said with more than a hint of wonder. Then her chin dipped to her chest. "Most of the pages were ripped out. Wait. Look at the last page." Her voice grew excited. "It says, 'Must rush out. There's no more time. Dr. Dragas will never find the image of the virus. He can track me down. But I don't have it. He'll never find it in my lab. Only ghosts. I must go . . .' Then the rest is just a scrawl."

"What does she mean by 'only ghosts'?" I wondered aloud.

Elijah leaned in to inspect. "Maybe because the page is torn up, like a ghost of a page?"

"I doubt it," said Jeremy.

"Well," said Phoenix, "I bet Dr. Franklin had to hurry away to evade that horrible Dr. Dragas. There probably wasn't enough time for her to transport the virus image out of the lab without real danger."

"I bet she was worried about Dr. Dragas finding her and taking the image if she kept it with her," said Elijah.

"That image has to be somewhere in here," said Memito, his eyes scanning the shelves. "It says so in the journal. Blanche said it's up to us to find it before Dragas gets here."

"We already know most of this," said Jeremy, groaning impatiently. "Dr. Franklin obviously hid that image. Now it's time to find more clues. So we can get out of here in time."

Memito set down the timer with a plunk on the counter in front of him. "Guys, we only have thirty-eight minutes. I couldn't even take my shower and get ready for school in that amount of time. Just saying."

Birdie glanced at the front door longingly. "Seems like a long time."

"Not really," said Jeremy. "Let's find some more clues."

I hurried to a central lab table and checked if anything might be hidden underneath. Even after swiping my fingers on the backs of some stools, I came up with nothing. Not even a ball of dust was in sight on the neatly swept floor.

Meanwhile Birdie stood across from me inspecting the back of a chalkboard. Memito spun a globe of the world with his finger and then shook it to see if anything was inside. Elijah fiddled with the buttons on an old-fashioned radio that had a glowing yellow tube coming out the top of it. "It really looks like we've stepped back in time," he said.

"I know." Memito joined Elijah, who was now sliding his hand around the back of the radio. "Man, that thing is old," said Memito. "What if it breaks? And then you'd have to use your allowance to pay for it. Or what if—"

"—there is a hidden code inside of *this.*" Elijah pulled an instruction booklet from behind the radio.

"Is there food behind there, too?" asked Memito. "I'm starving."

"Hey, I just found a receipt," Birdie announced. "It was behind a picture frame. It's for a plane trip somewhere." She squinted thoughtfully. "Unfortunately, the print is too faded."

"Good. Good!" I encouraged. "We do know that Rosalind Franklin left on a trip."

"More clues isn't always better," mumbled Jeremy. "That could be a red herring. Something to throw us off. We need to find something that will lead to that." He pointed to the lock on the door.

"And that image of the virus," Phoenix reminded us. Kneeling down in front of the main door, she flipped over a small area rug. "You never know what could help." She pulled off a tag. "This wasn't attached. It could be something."

"Probably not," said Jeremy.

"You guys," I said, waving my arms in a stop motion. "Hold up. We have to have a plan."

Jeremy stepped next to me. "Yeah. You're right."

I couldn't believe he was actually agreeing with me. I met Birdie's eyes in a look of astonishment.

"My brother loves watching escape room hacks on YouTube," said Jeremy "So I've seen a ton of them. One of the number one tips is to have a project manager." He thumped his chest. "That's me."

"Actually, I think it should be me," I said. "Since I probably know the most about"—I spun around the lab—"all the equipment in this place."

"Yes, but did you watch the top ten escape room tips video?" said Jeremy. "No." He pointed to the egg timer. "You hear that thing ticking? Well, we only have thirty-six—correction, thirty-five—minutes. The trick is to divide and conquer." He waved his arms. "And put all the clues in one place. Let's say right here." He grabbed a flashlight off a tabletop, clicked it on, and flicked the light over the surface. "This can be the official clue corner. It's next to a whiteboard and dry erase pen. Obviously to help us write down codes, if we ever find any."

"Okay," I said, a little reluctantly. "It does make sense." That's when I spotted a plain white piece of paper sitting on top of the desk.

I snatched the sheet. "This could be a clue. What if it came from the journal?"

"Then it goes on the clue table," directed Jeremy.

"Okay. Fine." I dropped the sheet down onto the table and double-checked to make sure I wasn't missing any teeny-tiny writing or something.

"Kate, I hope you know the paper is blank," said Memito.

"Hey, I know," snorted Jeremy. "The message on the blank piece of paper is: *Help. I'm a snowman in a snowstorm.*" He cracked up. Nobody else laughed, except for Memito, who gave a little chuckle.

"You guys, there could be a secret message," I said in all seriousness. "It could be written with lemon juice. I saw that done on Dr. Caroline's YouTube show once." As I waved the flashlight over the paper, I felt a quiver of excitement. "Wait for it, you guys."

On second thought, wait for nothing. The paper just remained blank. No secret codes. No numbers or letters.

Frustrated, I clicked to make the light bright.

Still nothing.

"I was so sure," I said, biting my lip. "I mean, what's the point of having a completely blank piece of paper?"

"Not much. Knew it wouldn't work," said Jeremy.

"Maybe it's just to write on?" suggested Birdie.

"Doubtful," said Phoenix. "Remember, we have that whiteboard and markers."

Suddenly, Jeremy hurried over to the shelf right above the clue table. "Hey, you guys. I think I just found the answer. Crayons."

"Why would a world-famous scientist have crayons in her lab?" I said.

"That makes no sense." Phoenix shrugged.

"Well, exactly. That's why it's a clue." Jeremy snatched a red crayon. "Let's rub it over the paper and see if it works. I saw Dr. Caroline do that to a salt-infused paper. The salt crystals collect more crayon wax, revealing a secret message!"

"I've never heard of that," I harrumphed. "But I guess it's worth a try." I motioned for Birdie to come over. "You should do it, Birdie. You have the artistic touch."

"Uh, sure. I mean, anyone can use a crayon. But why not?" Birdie rubbed the crayon over the paper.

"Wow, it took two of you guys to figure out how to use a crayon," said Jeremy, shaking his head.

"Shh! Something is showing up!" said Birdie.

"A coil-looking thingy," said Elijah. "Right on the paper.

"I see! I see!" I couldn't help but jump up and down. "And lots of numbers. 020-7111-2413."

"That's a code!" said Jeremy, who sounded truly excited for the first time.

"Try the number on the front door," said Elijah.

When Jeremy grabbed the paper with the numbers, I didn't try to snag it back. There was no way I was going to get into another tug-of-war with him.

Jeremy studied the lock and exhaled loudly. "Nope. Won't work. This lock is one of those four-number combination ones."

"Great. I don't see any other locks," said Memito, scanning the lab. "Or snacks in this place. I'm so hungry."

"I thought this was going to be easy," said Jeremy with a frustrated groan.

"Well, guess again," I said.

CHAPTER FOURTEEN

THE LADDER TO SOMEWHERE

Double Helix (noun). The appearance of a double-stranded DNA molecule with two lines that run parallel to each other and twist together. DNA is very famous and probably would have signed autographs if it could have.

"WE DIDN'T FIND ANYTHING in the bathroom," Elijah said as he and Memito stepped out of the tiny bathroom on the side of the PTA office. We continued to search through the lab, opening drawers and looking behind bookshelves. There were lots of books on molecular chemistry. But no textbook on DNA since Rosalind Franklin had just made that breakthrough. Understanding the structure of DNA might have been the most important discovery of the twentieth century. At least, that's what Dr. Caroline says. DNA is a molecule that looks like a twisted ladder. That's why they call it the double helix. DNA is sort of like an instruction booklet for your body to do every job it needs to survive. It tells each cell in your body what it needs to do, like telling your hair how to grow or your stomach how to break down food.

Suddenly thoughts of DNA gave me an idea. "Hey, you guys, you know that coil that appeared after we rubbed the crayon on the paper? What if it's DNA? Maybe it's another clue."

"But it's not like we can see DNA with our eyes," said Phoenix.

"True," I said. "You can't even see DNA with a regular microscope. It's ridiculously small."

Somehow before we knew it, we had twenty-nine minutes left. Actually, it was hard to forget since Memito kept on reminding us every few minutes.

"Hey, look at that old-timey phone," said Memito suddenly, pointing to a high-up shelf. It was black with a rotary dial. "I just noticed it. And there's some kind of letter next to it."

"Yeah, and the phone's got a really long coil thingy," said Elijah.

I whirled around to stare up at the phone and an old-fashioned curly telephone cord. I pumped my fist in the air. "Score! A coil. That's our clue."

"Wow. It really does look just like the coil on the paper," said Birdie, amazed.

"Quick! Quick, get it down," I yelled.

"Ugh, where's Skyler when you need him?" said Elijah as he tried to jump up to reach the phone and the letter, but it was just out of reach.

"Use the stepladder," said Phoenix, pointing to a small ladder in the corner.

I grabbed it and shoved it against the bookcase.

In a flash, Elijah climbed up a couple of rungs and pulled down the phone, along with the envelope. "There's a cardboard tube here, too," he exclaimed. After taking the plastic cap off the tube, he inspected it and shrugged. "It's empty." He stuck it in his lab coat pocket. "This will make a great drumstick though." Then he ripped open the envelope and began to read the note.

"Customers, please pardon the interruption in service. There was an explosion nearby that knocked out the wires. But service has been restored." Then he flipped to the back of the note. "There's a zero next to an eleven, then the number forty-four written in giant numbers." He shrugged. "Maybe it's how much the stationery cost?"

"Listen to the phone," said Elijah. "Maybe there's a message for us."

Memito picked up the phone's receiver. "Nah, it's dead. Dead like we're going to be if we don't escape this room and that evil dude gets here, Dr. Dragon."

"Dragas," corrected Phoenix.

"Can you not use the word 'dead,'" I pleaded.

"The point is that an old-timey-looking phone has no dial tone," said Jeremy.

"And can you not say 'old-timey,'" said Phoenix. "It takes us out of the moment."

"Then why do you dress that way?" accused Jeremy, nodding at Phoenix's vintage shirt. "All old-timey?"

"Everyone, please stop arguing," said Birdie, her voice warbling. "I seriously want to get out of here." Her eyes slid to the combination lock on the front door.

"Birdie is right," I said. "We need to find the image of the virus and figure out the code to open the lock."

"Also, anything can be a code," Jeremy stated with certainty.

"Yeah," agreed Memito. "I once saw this video where kids were trapped in an escape room. I mean really stuck because it was a horror movie. And anyhow, they had to deal with this creepy guy in a clown outfit if they wanted to live."

"Oh, please stop," I said, clapping my hands over my ears. "I really don't want to hear about creepy clowns."

"Me either," said Birdie.

"We should also think about what might be a safe or even a lock," said Jeremy. "In this one escape room I heard about, the roulette wheel was actually this giant combination lock. So everyone keep your eyes open."

Memito opened his eyes extra wide. "I'm looking!" he shouted.

"Hey, what about that telephone?" I said, pointing to the old black phone with a rotary dial. "Maybe it's not a phone, but a safe."

"Yes!" agreed Elijah. "It's got to be here for a reason."

I lifted up the phone and examined it. "This could

be a lock. What was that number again? The one on the blank paper?"

"I'll read it," said Phoenix. "020-7111-2413."

"That's too long for a combination lock," said Jeremy. "Remember?"

"What if it's a phone number?" said Phoenix, her voice growing excited.

"Okay, um, how do you dial one of these?" asked Memito. "It kind of scares me."

"It's easy," said Elijah. "My grandpa has a bunch of old phones. He keeps them for fun. You dial with the wheel. And pick up this thingy from that thingy."

I shook my head. "Oh, wow. You and directions." Elijah was notorious for throwing away his Lego set directions.

"It's called removing the handset from the cradle," said Phoenix. "I know because when I was younger, I

read old Nancy Drew books."

Memito put the handset up to his ear. "It's still dead."

"Put your finger in the hole of the number you want to dial," explained Elijah. "Then make the dial thingy go clockwise until it hits the metal thingy."

Memito started dialing as I called out the numbers.

Then we all held our collective breath.

"Nothing," said Memito. He looked up with his hands raised in the *why me* position.

"Maybe it's the wrong number," said Elijah.

"Let Phoenix try," said Jeremy. "Since she's old-timey."

Phoenix marched up to Memito, swung her waist-length hair, and grasped the phone. "Thank you very much," she said in her polite manner. She lifted up the handset very slowly and dialed the number. *Click. Click. Click. Click.*

Then she nodded. "Uh-huh." She nodded again. "Thank you very much," she said, putting down the phone.

"Were you actually speaking to somebody?" asked Elijah.

"Well, yes," said Phoenix.

"Who?" asked Jeremy, his voice rising in excitement.

Phoenix smiled serenely. "Rosalind Franklin, of course."

"You can't listen to the real Rosalind Franklin," said

Memito, shaking his head. "She died a long time ago."

"It could be her ghost then," said Elijah in a spooky voice.

Memito blew out his cheeks to make creepy wind sound effects. Even though it was a joke, a tingle crawled up my spine.

"True, it could be a ghost," said Birdie. I love my best friend, but that's an area where we disagree. And while I don't believe in ghosts, I still don't want to think about them.

I must have been wincing, because Jeremy wiggled his fingers and started going, "Boooooooooooo. I'm going to haunt you, Kate."

"Ha ha ha," I said. "You're so hysterical."

That's when Phoenix waved her hand. "Confession. The phone was dead. I was just saying that to have a little fun. Maybe it won't work since my grandma said that a long time ago, phone numbers in London were shorter and had letters."

Jeremy gave a bark of a laugh. "Wow. I didn't know you made jokes, Phoenix. I thought you were serious all the time."

"That's because you're seriously unobservant," said

Phoenix, her lips curving up into a gloating sort of smile.

"Actually, I'm very observant." Jeremy folded his arms. "During the Science Challenge, I held on to the water bottle for like two seconds, and I got slammed for it." He glared at Phoenix. "When you throw a napkin, what happens? Nothing." He shook his head.

"Can you guys stop this?" begged Elijah. "We're supposed to be a team."

"It's sort of hard with Jeremy," I confessed. "If it were up to him, we'd be locked in detention instead of an escape room. That's just plain weird."

"I almost wanted that detention because I wanted to see Phoenix get in trouble for once," huffed Jeremy.

"That's the most ridiculous thing I've ever heard," I said.

Phoenix swished to stand closer to Jeremy. "If you have something to say to me, Jeremy, you should just say it. Just be direct."

"Okay, fine," he replied.

"Thanks for at least telling me how you feel," said Phoenix.

Jeremy said under his breath so you could hardly hear, "Yeah, well, I'm glad you at least listened."

I could feel the tension in the room start to lift away, sort of like effusion in chemistry. That's when gas particles escape and go somewhere else.

"We're supposed to be a team. So let's do that," I said.

Suddenly, Phoenix snapped her fingers. "The numbers on the back of the note! That's how you call Great Britain from the United States. You dial the 011 to exit the U.S., then 44 to connect with Great Britain, *then* we dial the regular phone number." She shook her head. "How did we miss that? We just learned about exit codes and country codes in social studies!"

"The country code, 44, for Great Britain makes sense," I said, "since that's where Rosalind Franklin was from!"

"Exactly." Phoenix held out the receiver. "I have an idea. Let's try the phone again. But this time let's add in the country code for Great Britain. And the exit code, 011, from the U.S."

"Brilliant!" I grabbed the receiver. "I'll listen, but why don't you dial, since you know what to do, Phoenix."

"Sure." Phoenix shrugged.

"We're wasting time," moaned Jeremy. "We've already gone over this."

"Third time's the charm."

"We don't have time to do this over again. We don't need to do things double," grumbled Jeremy.

"It's good to be sure," stated Birdie.

"No, it's good to move on," huffed Jeremy.

"Yeah," said Memito, glancing at the egg timer, "because now we only have twenty-two minutes. I don't know if we can make it, guys."

"Everyone, please stop just standing around watching." Jeremy glanced at the ticking timer. "We're wasting time."

I bounced on my toes impatiently while Phoenix once again dialed. I had to hold myself back from yelling at her to hurry.

Suddenly, Phoenix was handing me the phone. And I put the earpiece to my ear. It was as cold as ice on my skin.

And that's when Rosalind Franklin started speaking.

CHAPTER FIFTEEN

ON THE TABLE

The Periodic Table (noun). A chart listing elements in order of their atomic number. The atomic number is the number of itty-bitty particles called protons in each atom. And just like fingerprints are unique to each human, the atomic number is unique for each element.

A VOICE I ASSUMED WAS ROSALIND FRANKLIN'S was whispering in my ear. But no, it couldn't be. Because the voice coming from the handset sounded creepy and said, "Hellooooo. I must warn you there's a ghost. A ghost in the WC. Be very careful." I set down the receiver. My heart beat a million times per second.

"So?" asked Phoenix. "Did you hear anything?"

"Something that could help?" asked Birdie.

"Not to me," I stated.

94

"Figures," said Jeremy.

Then I motioned Phoenix and Birdie to follow me over by the corner. "Look, I heard a voice on the phone. A really spooky one," I whispered. "And it gave me the creeps. But I think that was the only point."

"What did it say?" asked Phoenix.

I closed my eyes and sighed. "That there's a ghost in the lab. And for us to be very careful. Actually, it said the ghost was in the WC." I shrugged. "Whatever that is. I bet the idea was just to scare Dragas. You know, that bad guy."

"But what's a WC?" asked Birdie.

"That's what people in England call the bathroom," said Phoenix in a loud dramatic whisper. "It stands for water closet!"

Jeremy stomped over to us and stopped in front of Phoenix. "I heard everything you all were saying," he said.

"Me too," said Elijah, and his voice sounded a little hurt. Memito nodded.

"You shouldn't keep secrets," said Elijah.

"I think Kate should be the one to go into the haunted water closet," said Jeremy. "To check it out."

"Fine," I said, but I didn't feel fine. My heart was pounding. And my mouth felt dry.

"I'll go with you," whispered Birdie, who could obviously tell I was just a little freaked out.

A moment later, we creaked open the door to the water closet. Birdie shone a light so it wouldn't be so dark.

"I hear something," I said, whirling around.

"It's called pipes. It's normal," said Birdie as she flicked on the light switch. The cramped WC remained dark.

"Of course there's no light bulb," I said. "The idea is to completely terrify us, so our brains don't work. Birdie, I'm so glad you're with me right now. I hope you're no longer mad at me."

"Me mad at you? What gave you that idea?"

"You've just been so quiet and acting a little different."

"Because I'm afraid of small spaces," she whispered. "And we're locked in an escape room."

"Then why are you here with me right now?" I asked. "The WC is extra small."

"Because you're my best friend and you're afraid

of ghosts. And we've got to catch one in here."

"Aw, Birdie," I said, giving her a hug. "You're the best, seriously."

"Thanks, Kate. Right back at you. If anything, I thought you might be upset with me."

Birdie opened the drawers under the sink. "It's probably dumb to look since Elijah and Memito were already here." She shrugged. "But they might have missed something."

I shone the light over a roll of toilet paper that was randomly covered in plastic wrap. "So please explain why you think I might possibly be mad at you?"

"Because I'm the one who got us in trouble. I spent all the time picking out colors and got us behind during the Fall Science Challenge. If we hadn't been behind, then you wouldn't have gotten in a mood and done the tug-of-war with Jeremy—"

"That's ridiculous. You're not to blame." I tapped my chest. "*Me*. I'm the one. I totally forgot the most important rules in a lab: be careful, and no fighting. I have to learn to be patient." I wiped my forehead. I was actually sweating as if I had been running. "I'm really nervous," I admitted.

"Me too," said Birdie.

"That's because you believe in ghosts."

She shook her head. "No, because I was worried about . . . us."

I put my arm around her shoulders. "No way. We're best friends and—"

"What's that?" asked Birdie, pointing to a small gray appliance sitting on a shelf across from the faucet.

I strode over and cautiously picked it up. "Looks like a cross between a hair dryer and a watering can." Running my fingers along the base, I found an on-off switch. "I wonder what it does?"

"I'm not sure.

"It looks familiar. And yet not so much."

Birdie snapped her fingers. "It's a steamer. My nani uses it to quickly dewrinkle her clothes when she travels for work." Nani is Birdie's grandma on her mom's side.

She's an economist and sometimes travels to confer-ences. Economists use numbers to predict trends in the economy, like sales.

Right now, if I had to make a prediction based on numbers, I'd say things were looking shaky. And then Memito shouted, "Fourteen minutes!"

That didn't give us much time to figure things out!

CHAPTER SIXTEEN

GHOSt BUSteRS

Distilled Water (noun). Steam that has been trapped from boiling water and then condensed back into water. This water is super pure because it doesn't have stuff like calcium and iron in it. Basically, all the minerals are heavier than water so they stay in the pot of boiling water.

NEXT TO THE STEAMER WAS a giant bottle of distilled water. Distilled water is frequently used in science labs. "I bet that's why Ms. Daly had a bottle on her desk. Remember? We need to use it to turn water into steam."

Distilled Water

With my fingers, I traced along the body of the steamer to see if anything easily popped open. With a snap, the top came off. "Oh, there's already water in here," I said, feeling excited.

Grabbing the plug, Birdie jammed it into the outlet. A blue light turned on.

"Hurry up, hurry up!" I cried. "We only have about thirteen minutes."

"Did you find anything?" asked Jeremy, peeking through the doorway.

"We've made a discovery," said Birdie. "This thing should only take a minute or two to heat up. We need it."

"It's a steamer," I explained.

The steamer began sputtering and coughing.

"Oh no. Is it broken?" asked Jeremy.

"It does that right before it's ready," said Birdie.

Steam puffed out, curling upward. "It's like a ghost," I shrieked. "Oh. Wow. This is the ghost. A ghost is in the WC!"

"Great," said Jeremy. "We already did the Ghost demo." He waved his flashlight so a disk of yellow light bobbed up and down.

"Wait," I said to Jeremy. "Do that again."

"Do what again?" he asked.

101

"Wave the flashlight over the mirror. I thought I saw something." He stepped farther into the WC. And there on the mirror was a secret message. It said *2 pockets*.

"Wow. That's cool," Jeremy said.

Birdie and I looked at each other in pure astonishment.

"The steam revealed the letters!" I cried. "Someone must have written the message with their bare hands, and then the steam condensed around the oils left from their fingers! Just like the phone said. A ghost in the WC! We found another clue."

"That's great," said Jeremy. "We've got to find two pockets!"

The three of us raced back into the lab. "We've got to find pockets," Birdie repeated.

Everyone checked their lab coat pockets. But nobody found anything. We even checked our jeans pockets. I spun around the lab, "Does anyone see any pockets?"

"I think I might," said Memito. He pulled out a little green spiral pad from the bookshelf. "A pocket notebook."

Jeremy high-fived him. "You rock."

Memito flipped through the pages. He shrugged. "I dunno. Just a bunch of equations that make no sense."

"Those numbers could be the key to cracking the code." I waved at the lock on the front door. "And getting us out of here."

Elijah flipped through some more pages. "Hey, there's a message." He held it up and in big block letters it said, YOU'LL NEVER FIND THE IMAGE OF THE VIRUS.

"That's not a happy thought," said Birdie, glancing longingly at the very locked front door.

"Wait. What if that message wasn't for us?" said Phoenix. "What if it was for the bad guy, Dragas? Rosalind Franklin left clues for us so we could hand the image of the virus over to Blanche before Dragas gets here. But she couldn't make the clues obvious. Otherwise—" she shook her head. "The virus could get into the wrong hands."

"Wait. Hold up," said Memito. "On the very last page, there's one word over and over." He jabbed his finger onto the paper. "Tube."

I snapped my fingers. "Like test tubes, I bet." Then I groaned. "But I've checked every test tube in the lab."

103

"Yeah," said Elijah, staring at the cardboard tube he had kept for a drumstick. The one he had spotted by the telephone. "Guess what, I think I just found something!" He opened the cardboard tube by pulling off the plastic cap, then pulled out a rolled-up something white. "I didn't see it before because it's so thin." He flattened the image, which looked like a photograph, and Jeremy shone the flashlight on it so we could see even better in the dim room.

There was a gray image of what looked like a pile of some weird sticks.

"The image of the virus!" I shouted, high-fiving Elijah. "You're a genius."

Birdie gazed at the image with a look of wonder. "Who knew that viruses could look like . . . art."

Then Elijah flipped the image over. "Look, there's a code on the back, just like the note!"

"Read it aloud!" shouted Phoenix. "And I'll write it on the whiteboard."

"32-73-5-57-19-3-52," called out Elijah, and then rolled the image back into the tube. "I'll put it here for safekeeping." He stuffed the tube back in the right pocket of his lab coat.

"We did it!" I shouted.

"Not quite," said Jeremy. "We still need to get out of here. And the clue in the WC said two pockets. We need to find another pocket."

Memito held up the stopwatch. "The clock is ticking. We now only have ten minutes!"

"We've got to get going," I admitted.

But Birdie didn't move from her spot. Instead, she stared dreamily at the periodic table on the wall. "You know, I think it'd be cool to have one of those in my room. But to make some art project out of it."

"Okaaaaay," said Jeremy. "I think we're getting way off track here." For once, I knew exactly how Jeremy felt. Right now was not the time to think about room decorations.

"There are numbers there," Birdie said. "And some of them are just like the numbers in the secret message on that paper."

I snapped my fingers so hard I thought I could light a fire. "Birdie, that's amazing! That could be it. Each element on the periodic table has a number. For example, oxygen or O is the eighth element. That's why there's a number eight over it."

Phoenix wiped the whiteboard clean and winced. "Okay, let's try this out."

"Does your hand still hurt?" Birdie asked.

She shook her head. "I'm fine."

I glanced up at the periodic table. "The number thirty-two is germanium. That's Ge," I said in a rush.

Phoenix wrote that down.

"And seventy-three is Ta, which stands for tantalum."

"Got it," said Phoenix.

"The fifth element is boron. B," said Jeremy.

"Fifty-seven is lanthanum or La," I said. "And nineteen is potassium, K. Number three is lithium, which is Li. And finally, fifty-two is tellurium, which is Te."

We all stood there scanning the letters to see if we could made sense of them.

"It's says "GeTaBLaKLiTe," said Birdie, shaking her head.

"Oh, that's so helpful." Jeremy laughed. "Sounds like gibberish or some alien language."

Birdie sighed heavily. "I really thought . . ."

"No, you thought right, Birdie," I said. "We have to just keep on figuring it out."

Jeremy stepped away to start inspecting some test tubes.

Elijah came over to look at the letters with me, Birdie, and Phoenix.

"That says 'Get,'" Phoenix pointed out.

And then Elijah's mouth dropped open. "It says 'Get a blak lite'! We need to find a black light!"

I could feel the smile stretching across my face. And we all jumped up and down. Now we were really fired up!

CHAPTER SEVENTEEN

THE LIGHT WILL SET US FREE

Mercury (noun). One of two elements that is a liquid at room temperature. It moves around like an alien and it's super shiny—you could almost imagine it's from the planet Mercury!

"OKAY, IT'S SIMPLE NOW," said Jeremy. "We just need to find a black light."

"On it," I said, kneeling on the floor to search under the desk.

Birdie went back to inspecting the bookshelf.

Elijah banged open and shut every drawer, while Memito inspected behind various doors. And Jeremy checked behind some framed posters.

My eyes scanned the tile floor for something we had missed. I picked up area carpets as Birdie slid her hands behind the old radio to check it out one more time.

Suddenly there was shuffling outside. "Please, hurry!" said the spy formerly known as Ms. Daly. "Dr. Dragas and his gang are almost at the lab. You're running out of time."

"Guys, we can do this!" said Elijah, staring at the clock.

"Only eight more minutes," reported Memito. His voice sounded as panicked as I felt. He plopped onto a seat. "I don't see how we can get out in time before . . . you-know-who arrives."

I frantically scanned the lab. Could there be a black light clue near one of the gazillion test tubes? No, we had already checked. Or maybe in the bookshelf? No. It had been thoroughly searched as well. "The answer has to be here somewhere. I'm sure we're missing something big."

"Kate's right," said Jeremy. And for a moment, I blinked in complete shock. Did Jeremy Rowe just agree with me for the second time today? I felt too stunned to say anything back.

"Hey, what if it's something right in front of our

eyes," added Jeremy. "Something so obvious it's funny."

That's when Elijah started grinning really big. He raced into the closet and pulled out a blue lab coat. He dug his hands into the left pocket of it and whipped out what looked like a thick black pen. "Look what I found!"

"Dude, how?" asked Memito. "We already checked those coats."

"I know," said Elijah. "I put on the lab coat I'm wearing now when we first got here. The one I got in Daly's lab was too small. Ms. Daly must have planted this blacklight in my pocket."

Memito smacked his head. "That's why we didn't find it. Because you had already switched lab coats."

"Yup!" Elijah clicked the back of the light, and suddenly Jeremy's white shirt was glowing super bright. "It's you!" joked Elijah. "Jeremy is the message."

"You know it, bay-bee!" said Jeremy.

Phoenix and I snickered. The light hit a bar of soap near the faucet in the WC. I raced over to pick it up to see if any message was on it. It was so bright it almost looked radioactive in the dim room.

But nothing.

Elijah continued to shine the black light around the room, but nothing else was glowing, except for some paper on the desk, which we had already examined.

"It doesn't seem to be doing anything," I said, exasperated.

"Seven minutes," announced Jeremy, shining his regular flashlight on the timer.

Meanwhile, Memito started to try to open up the drawers in a cabinet.

"I've looked through those," Jeremy huffed.

"Well, you didn't find this." Memito held up a ball of black slime and threw it for Elijah to catch.

"Gross," said Elijah. He set it down on a nearby table.

"Why would Dr. Franklin have slime in her lab?" asked Phoenix as she started opening drawers on the desk.

"I've already done that," said Memito.

"Well, you didn't open this center drawer." Phoenix tapped the drawer right under the desktop. "Because it's stuck."

Memito pulled on the knob. "Because it's supposed to be that way. It's one of those fake drawers."

Crouching down, Jeremy inspected. "Nope. They

usually only do those fake drawers in bathrooms. They're directly under the sink. An actual drawer assembly can't fit because of all the plumbing."

"Wow. I didn't know that," admitted Elijah as Jeremy began to try to pry open the drawer.

"My uncle is a plumber." Jeremy shrugged. "He's taken me to a few jobs." He tugged on the knob. "This is a real drawer all right. I could probably do something if I could just work the blade of a putty knife right down in there." He continued to try to pull.

"Whoa, stop," I said. "Remember what Ms. Daly—I mean that spy said. We shouldn't force anything."

"I think the drawer might have a magnet inside," said Jeremy.

Memito started counting down the minutes. "Five minutes. That's all we got."

"Stop," said Birdie. "You're making me nervous."

Crouching down, I shone a flashlight in the little crack in the drawer. "I don't see a magnet," I said. "I don't know what you're talking about."

"Me either," said Elijah.

Then I remembered something I saw on *Dr. Caroline*, and suddenly, it all made sense.

CHAPTER EIGHTEEN

SLiMeD!

Adhesion (noun). This is the force that binds molecules together. And it's the reason why iron filings don't slip right out of magnetic slime.

"MAGNETIC SLIME!" I scooped up the black blob on the desktop. "That stuff has iron in it, which is magnetic. I just watched Dr. Caroline make magnetic slime with iron oxide, glue, and borax last week."

And Ms. Daly had a bottle of iron oxide powder on her desk back in her lab!

The blob oozed between my fingers and felt awesome and gross at the same time. I pressed it against the drawer.

It stuck right to it. "Jeremy was right about the magnet," I said. "But I have no clue what to do next."

"The plastic wrap!" screamed Birdie. She zipped into the WC and sprinted back into the lab, removing the plastic wrap from the toilet paper as she ran. Palming the slime, she wrapped it in the plastic and tossed it to Elijah.

"What are you doing?" asked Memito.

"No questions," begged Jeremy, pointing at the timer. "Two minutes."

My heart thudded so loudly it could probably be heard clear across the school.

Elijah used the magnetic slime, now wrapped up in plastic, to slide the magnet in the drawer to the left.

The drawer opened!

Waving my flashlight, we all peered inside. But there was nothing.

"It's empty!" moaned Memito slapping his hands against his forehead. "We're running out of time."

"This is so bad," said Jeremy.

"We're not getting out," said Birdie with a dramatic sigh.

"We can!" I cheered, but honestly, I wasn't so sure. In fact, I was really starting to doubt it.

"Hey, nobody talk for a second," said Elijah. "Let's think."

"The black light!" shouted Phoenix.

I grabbed the light off the table.

There were only sixty seconds left.

CHAPTER NINETEEN

TiME IS UP

Phosphors (noun). Substances that glow when struck by special kinds of light, such as ultraviolet light. Your teeth and fingernails have phosphors, which is why they look so awesome under a black light.

I SHONE THE LIGHT IN THE DRAWER. Glowing letters immediately appeared.

RIO.

"Rio! Is that some kind of element?" asked Birdie.

"Nope," I said.

"That's where Dr. Franklin went," guessed Phoenix. "It's in South America, Brazil, actually."

"Okay, great," said Jeremy. "Now we know where she's hiding out. What next?"

"That's where the globe comes in," said Phoenix. She

spun the globe until her finger hovered right over Brazil.

"Is there a code written on the globe?" asked Elijah hopefully.

"Maybe so," said Phoenix.

I sped over to the lock. "Latitude and longitude. Read them out," I said. "The longitude goes up and down the earth, just like how we cut an apple. And the latitude goes around the earth, like a hula hoop."

"Okay," called out Phoenix. "Wait. The latitude and longitude are written in Sharpie right here. That makes it easy, which is good since we don't have much time. The latitude is 22.91 and the longitude is 43.17."

"So that would be too many numbers," I called out. "This is a four-digit combination padlock."

"Try twenty-three and then forty-three," suggested Memito.

I swirled the numbers. I tried 2343. "Nope."

"What if you add the latitude and longitude together?" said Elijah, who loved math. "So it would be 6608. Try that!"

I spun the numbers into place and then tugged. The lock opened! We all burst out of the room, with four seconds to spare.

"We did it!" I cried, jumping up and down.

In the hallway, Blanche greeted us with a huge smile. And it grew even bigger as Elijah handed her the tube with the virus image. "For safekeeping," he said.

"Thank you. Dragas will never get it now," Blanche said, tucking it into her trench coat.

Then she took off her sunglasses and smiled with pride. "Really, congratulations, everyone. You did it! That was some wonderful teamwork!"

We all smushed into a group hug, jumping up and down.

"Does that mean that Dr. Dragas won't be able to rule the world?" asked Memito.

"That's right," said Ms. Daly. "You all saved the planet."

"And our grades," said Phoenix.

"I'll say," said Ms. Daly. "Those big fat goose egg zeroes have just been changed to hundreds. You guys used impressive teamwork in there, right down to the wire."

Birdie smiled at me. And I smiled back, giving her a knowing look and a wink.

"That was so much fun." Jeremy glanced at Phoenix, me, and Birdie. "You guys rocked."

Wow. Those were words I never thought I'd hear coming out of Jeremy Rowe's mouth.

"We all rocked," I said. And then we all high-fived each other.

"I don't think I'm going to be able to sleep very well tonight," admitted Memito. "Because my heart is never going to slow down."

"It's definitely a rush," I admitted. "So much science."

"And just plain fun!" yelled Elijah.

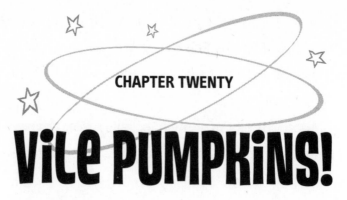

CHAPTER TWENTY

ViLe PUMPKiNS!

Catalyst (noun). Substances that speed up a chemical reaction by providing a better pathway from the reactants to the products. Think of them sort of like wilderness guides. They know all the shortcuts!

BACK IN THE LAB, Mom and Liam greeted me. "We've been anxiously waiting here hoping that you would get out on time," said Mom. "You did it. Congrats!"

"Thanks," I said. "I didn't realize you knew about the escape room the entire time." I bit my lip. "I should have told you about it."

"We can talk about it later," said Mom. "You know your father is going to want to have a long chat about this. It's not like you to keep anything from us. We did try to give you an opportunity at dinner to tell us."

I hung my head. "Yeah. I remember. I'm really sorry."

"I know," she said softly. "But it looks like you worked really hard to make it all right."

Liam hugged my waist. "You're alive!" he shrieked. "I thought you had gotten eaten by ghosts and monsters."

"Well, there was one ghost," I admitted, then explained about the steam cleaner.

"I'm glad it wasn't a real ghost and just a speriment," cried Liam.

"Experiment," corrected Mom with a smile.

"Yay! No ghosties!" yelled Liam.

Ms. Daly put her fingers to her lips. "Nobody can talk about what happened in the escape room. What happened in the lab stays in the lab."

"We don't want to spoil the surprise for the other kids," explained Mom.

Liam's lips curled down into a pout. "Now I know. And I'm a kid. I'll never get to go to an escape room."

Mom ruffled Liam's hair. "Don't be silly. When you're in fifth grade, Ms. Daly will make an escape room for you. And Daddy was talking about going to an escape room as a family. Maybe over winter break when we visit Grandma Dort and Grandpa Jack in Texas."

"Yay!" shrieked Liam. Then he looked at me with shining eyes. "You beat the bad guys."

"Thanks," I said. "But I wasn't so sure it would happen."

"Really?" said Birdie. "You seemed so confident."

"Well, I was literally sweating," I admitted.

"Me too," said Jeremy.

"Me three," said Memito.

"Me four," said Elijah.

"Me five," said Phoenix.

"Me six," said Birdie. "Big-time."

Ms. Daly announced, "I have an offer that I think you won't refuse. If you agree to work as a team again, you can make a second pumpkin vomit during the Fall Festival on Friday. Julia, Avery, and Skyler as the winners of the Fall Science Challenge will stand in front, but all of you can be up onstage, too. The winners from the other half of the class will be showcasing a glow-in-the-dark pumpkin later in the evening. And the rest of the kids will be demonstrating a drumming routine after that. So are you up for handling a Vomiting Pumpkin?"

Everyone looked at each other. "Yes!" we all shouted.

On Friday afternoon the Fall Festival had kicked off in a big way. And while kids and families could enjoy all kinds of booths, treats, and carnival games, we headed into the gym area for our show. That meant everyone from the escape room, plus Julia's group, of course. Basically, all the kids in our Fall Science Challenge group. Julia and I were carrying the jack-o'-lanterns. And, naturally, we were all wearing our lab coats, gloves, and goggles. Last night, with some help from Dad, I had carved my group's pumpkin with a giant mouth and big round eyes.

It was in the gym, so families could watch while they played some of the carnival games that were actually inside. There were all kinds of wonderful things laid out on a table for the silent auction, and they were even raffling off a bicycle. Plus, there was fun stuff like face and nail painting.

Phoenix looked a little sad when she spotted a craft table. "I want to make a bracelet for Avery," she said, "just like this one." She pointed to the macramé one on her wrist. She frowned. "But I can't because of my hand."

"That's okay, we'll help you later," said Birdie.

"Definitely," I said.

"You guys are the best," she said.

Up onstage, a group of first graders performed a falling leaves dance.

"So cute," gushed Birdie.

"I know it," said Julia. "It's hard to believe we were ever that little."

"I wasn't," said Skyler, and we all laughed, since he's always been the tallest boy, even in kindergarten.

"I can't believe Liam will be in first grade next year," I said. Each kid was dressed in golds, oranges, and yellows. They twirled around and sang a song about fluttering, falling leaves.

"Okay, once they're done," said Ms. Daly, "the fourth graders are going to sing a couple of songs out front, which gives me enough time to get all set up."

And before we knew it, we were walking onto the stage, ready to put on a truly disgusting show. As Ms. Daly promised, Julia's group was right up front and we were in the back, but I didn't mind. I was just happy to be up there doing science.

"We're going to be so gross," said Birdie, who stood on my right.

"Agreed," I said. "We're going to be disgusting."

"Vile," added Phoenix, standing directly to my left.

Avery, who was in front of Phoenix, gave a little twirl. Her short blonde braids twirled, too. "And sickening."

"Don't forget foul," said Julia from the front.

"The most gross, disgusting, vile, sickening, and foul ever," called out Jeremy from Birdie's right.

"Yeah!" shouted Memito and Elijah, who stood next to Jeremy.

"You're ready?" asked Ms. Daly.

"Definitely!" I said, pumping my fist into the air.

On the other side of the gym, there was a spooky cakewalk. Paper pumpkins had been cut out and taped to the floor in the gym for the spooky cakewalk path. Parents and kids were walking around the path while a volunteer dressed in an apple costume played "Monster Mash." But while our demo was going on, the apple stopped the cakewalk so everyone could watch.

I was so excited.

Ms. Daly cleared her throat and grabbed the microphone. "Are you ready for the Vomiting Pumpkins demo?" she asked.

The audience cheered. She pointed to our two tables.

"These pumpkins ate way too much candy last night, and now they are sick to their stomachs," said Ms. Daly, "so we're going to see what happens when you eat too much candy."

The audience cheered even louder.

"Okay, my teams onstage are now going to dump in their hydrogen peroxide," said Ms. Daly.

Jeremy grabbed a container of pre-measured hydrogen peroxide and poured it into a larger empty beaker. So did Julia.

"We're using thirty-five percent peroxide so it's more concentrated," continued Ms. Daly. "What you have at home is three to six percent. Now we're pouring in one cup of dish soap. And we decided that we wanted the vomit to be green, so we're going to put in food coloring."

Stepping next to me, Memito squeezed in some green food coloring from a small bottle.

"More more more!" I called out. "You can't have too much."

"That's right," said Ms. Daly. "We're looking for a beautiful homogenous mixture." I knew that meant that everything should be mixed together. "Now it's time to stir it up," continued Ms. Daly.

Avery and I picked up our beakers and swooshed them until they were all stirred. Some of the green liquid poured over the top and dribbled on my fingers. Luckily my fingers were safe because I was wearing my lab gloves (of course).

"Okay, I'll take those from you now." Ms. Daly placed my beaker in one of the jack-o'-lanterns. "It's important to put safety first. Always do science with a trained adult," said Ms. Daly. "I'm angling the beakers a bit just so we get some projectile vomiting."

I grinned as she put the awesomely yucky green mixture into the center of our pumpkin.

"Great job so far, everyone," exclaimed Ms. Daly as she finished placing Avery's beaker in her pumpkin. "What do you think, audience?" There were loud cheers. I could hear my dad whistling and see my mom and Liam wildly waving.

"One of the beakers moved!" Liam frantically pointed.

"That's okay," Ms. Daly assured him. "We're good. But that was a good observation. I'm glad you're on top of it. You're going to be a good scientist."

"Yay!" cried out Liam.

"Now I'm going to add the catalyst," said Ms. Daly. "A catalyst is sort of special, because it speeds up a chemical reaction. This catalyst is called potassium iodide."

I couldn't help but clap my hands. Catalysts are the best! I couldn't wait.

"Hopefully we'll see some vomit real soon," said Ms. Daly.

"Oh, yes!" I cried.

She started with Julia's pumpkin. After Ms. Daly added the catalyst to the beaker in the pumpkin, Julia quickly put the top back onto her jack-o'-lantern.

"Can you see it?" asked Ms. Daly. "Is it coming?"

"Oh my goodness! Yes," I shrieked.

Next she dumped the catalyst into my pumpkin.

"It's gross," yelled Memito and Elijah.

Foamy-looking sludge oozed out of the pumpkins' mouths.

"I love it! I love it!" I yelled.

"It's nice and disgusting," said Jeremy.

"It's definitely vile," said Phoenix.

"And sickening," sang out Julia, while Avery made a silly face.

"Can you see the heat that's coming off there?" asked Ms. Daly.

"Tons of it," said Elijah.

"It's an exothermic reaction," explained Ms. Daly. "So actually what happens is we use our catalyst to break down the hydrogen peroxide into oxygen and water. When it decomposes, the oxygen gas is trapped in the soap bubbles, which shoot out of the pumpkin in the form of vomit. It's a very hot reaction."

"That's so awesome," gushed some kids in the front row.

"That's science for you!" I shouted.

Later, Liam dragged Dad to the haunted bounce house, while Mom went to grab some hot cider. Birdie and I wound our way through the fair, buying candy apples, popcorn, and way too many other treats. We met up with Phoenix and Avery at the photo booth where we tried on silly hats, mustaches, and wigs.

Just as I was trying on a rainbow wig, Jeremy, Elijah, and Memito showed up. "Want to get in the photo?" I asked.

"Sure," said Elijah.

Jeremy and Memito both nodded. After they put on stuff to make them look like ridiculous scarecrows, we all laughed because Memito had so many lollipops jammed in his pockets.

"You're like a scarecrow that's stuffed with candy, dude," said Elijah.

"I can't help it," said Memito with a shrug. "I went to the lollipop pull and won."

"Everyone wins there," said Birdie, smiling.

"Speaking of winning," said Memito, pointing to the back of the gym. "Want to try and win something delicious at the cakewalk?"

"Oh yeah!" Jeremy rubbed his hands together. "And we should all do it together, at the same time."

"Awesome idea," said Elijah.

Birdie's eyes lit up. "That way we'll have a much better chance of winning."

"Plus, we can split the cake," suggested Phoenix.

"Yes," I shouted. "I love that idea!"

"Me too." Memito grinned and patted his stomach. "Especially chocolate cake."

"Chocolate is the best," I said. "But I think we should all do the cakewalk in costume."

"That might be a little scary," admitted Phoenix.

"That's all right," I said.

"Let's go," said Jeremy. "Ready, set, you bet."

And we all raced off to the gym together, screaming "boo" all the way.

MAGNETIC SLIME

Materials:

- ☆ ½ cup high-quality craft glue
- ☆ 4 tablespoons iron oxide powder
- ☆ ¼ cup saline solution
- ☆ 1 medium bowl
- ☆ 1 plastic spatula
- ☆ 1 neodymium bar magnet

Protocol:

1. Put on your safety goggles.

2. Pour glue into a medium bowl.

3. Have an adult help add the iron oxide powder to the glue.

   CAUTION: Do not breathe this in. Go outside to measure if you tend to spill things.

4. Stir the glue and powder until they're mixed together well.

5. Add saline solution to the mixture in the medium bowl.

6. Stir the glue mixture until all of the saline solution has been absorbed.

7. Allow the slime to sit for at least 3 minutes.

8. Wearing gloves, use your hands to knead the slime into a workable sphere.

   PRO TIP: Add a few drops of saline solution to your gloves to minimize the stickiness.

9. Use the neodymium magnet to play with the Magnetic Slime.

CAUTION: Watch your fingers if you have two magnets. You can easily pinch your fingers between these super-strong magnets.

HOW IT WORKS:

When we add the iron oxide powder directly to the glue, we see the adhesion forces at work. These forces only happen when one molecule has a strong attraction to a different molecule. Stirring the two chemicals together allows for the iron oxide to wiggle itself into the pockets of the polyvinyl acetate (glue). The cross-linked polymer forms when the glue and borate (saline) ions alternate, this time creating a creepy black ball of slime.

We added iron oxide to our slime because it is an extremely dense chemical that is magnetic at room temperature. This means that we can spike our slime with the black iron powder in order to give our gooey substance some magnetic properties. Copper and nickel are two other metals that do the same thing. In order to see the magnetic properties of iron, we have to use a neodymium magnet—traditional magnets are not strong enough to make the slime move!!

DR. Kate Biberdorf, also known as Kate the Chemist by her fans, is a science professor at UT-Austin by day and a science superhero by night (well, she does that by day, too). Kate travels the country building a STEM army of kids who love science as much as she does. You can often find her breathing fire or making slime—always in her lab coat and goggles.

You can visit Kate on Instagram and Facebook @KatetheChemist, on Twitter @K8theChemist, and online at KatetheChemist.com.